CW00855104

THE
MAGICAL
GATE

JULIE EARLE

Published by

MELROSE BOOKS

An Imprint of Melrose Press Limited
St Thomas Place, Ely
Cambridgeshire
CB7 4GG, UK
www.melrosebooks.co.uk

FIRST EDITION

Copyright © Julie Earle 2013

The Author asserts her moral right to
be identified as the author of this work

Cover designed by David Pearce

ISBN 978-1-908645-66-1

All rights reserved. No part of this publication may be reproduced, stored in a retrieval system, or transmitted, in any form or by any means electronic, mechanical, photocopying, recording or otherwise, without the prior permission of the publishers.

This book is sold subject to the condition that it shall not, by way of trade or otherwise, be lent, re-sold, hired out or otherwise circulated without the publisher's prior consent in any form of binding or cover other than that in which it is published and without a similar condition including this condition being imposed on the subsequent purchaser.

Printed and bound in Great Britain by:
Mimeo Ltd, Huntingdon, Cambridgeshire

FSC
www.fsc.org
MIX
From responsible
sources
FSC® C019549

Acknowledgements

I would like to thank all of my family for their continuing support. Without them this book would not have been possible, as they have been my encouragement all the way through. But most of all, I would like to thank my husband and children, who have been a constant blessing to me. They have listened to every part of this book and have encouraged me to go on—thanks, kids!

I would also like to thank Reece James Stevens for all his artwork. I would like say that everything written in this book is purely fiction, and has come from the author's own imagination.

Chapter One

IT WAS A BEAUTIFUL DAY, the sun was shining and the birds were singing. The forest looked so beautiful; it was amazing how the sun shone onto the glorious flowers and through the tall trees.

At the edge of the forest was a little stone house with a thatched roof and a little white picket fence all the way around the garden. In the house lived a family and a little girl called Amy.

Amy loved living in the forest. She loved looking at all the different flowers that grew out there, but she had only seen them when her parents had taken her out for a walk. Amy was never allowed to go out into the forest on her own to play as she was too young, but she longed for an adventure! She had never had one of those before. She felt like something was missing.

One day, as she was playing on her bicycle, something caught her eye; she noticed something sparkling at the bottom of her garden, and as she followed the sparkles, she came to a Gate, which she'd never seen before. I wonder where this came from, she thought, and as she moved closer to it, the sparkles stopped at the Gate. She knew she shouldn't leave her safe garden like her mum had told her so many times, but she wanted to know what was beyond the Gate. She just had to know what was sparkling. She could see the sparkles moving, going further into the forest. Her hand began to shake as she reached up to lift the metal latch, and as she lifted it her heart was racing with excitement and nerves all at the same time.

She slowly opened the Gate and stepped into the forest. It was like she had entered a different world, a world she had never seen or been to before; this wasn't the forest that she knew. She shrieked with excitement, "An adventure; how exciting!"

As she looked around she saw that the world she had just stepped into was the most beautiful place she had ever seen. The flowers were prettier and the trees were the most wonderful colours, the grass was pure green and the stream was like crystal; if you looked into it you could see yourself. Never before had she seen such beauty."Wow! Where am I?" she said.

Just then she heard a little voice say, "You're in Fairyland."

Amy jumped and looked around but could not see anyone there.

"Who said that? Hello, I said, who said that?"

"I did. I'm down here."

As Amy looked down she saw a very tiny but very beautiful fairy. She wore a red dress and her hair was golden like the sun; her wings were like silk that sparkled with jewels.

"You are so beautiful," Amy said. She remembered the sparkles she had seen. "Was that you I saw sparkling? Are you the sparkle fairy?"

The beautiful fairy let out a tiny but cute giggle. "Yes, my wings sparkle when the sun shines on them. I was playing with the bees in and out of the flowers. They take us to different places to help us collect our food, and they are our friends. My name is Cherry."

As Cherry turned to one side the sun caught her wings, which began to sparkle. She had so many pretty colours in them. Amy smiled and said, "Pleased to meet you." As she turned around she saw that the Magical Gate had disappeared. "Oh no! How am I going to get back? Now my mum will know for sure that I have disobeyed her. I am going to get into so much trouble when I get home."

Cherry looked at Amy and said, "Don't worry, the Gate appears again at sunset. Until then let me show you Fairyland. You will love it."

Cherry

As they walked through the forest Amy couldn't help noticing how the trees were so much greener and the grass was so beautiful, the sky was light blue and the clouds were fluffy. She had never seen clouds like that before; she could almost touch them.

"WOW! This is so wonderful."

"If you think this is beautiful you should see Fairyland itself. This is just the beginning."

"You mean there's more?"

"Much more," Cherry said.

They stopped at a little hole in the ground. Amy looked at Cherry and said, "I'll never fit in there, I'm too big."

Cherry couldn't help but giggle and said, "Trust me, come on and slide down this hole, and be prepared to be amazed."

As Amy took Cherry's tiny little hand her heart was racing with excitement. What will I see, and who will I meet? she thought.

Amy

As they jumped into the hole, to Amy's surprise it expanded to her size. Pure excitement ran through Amy as they both landed at the bottom. Amy landed on the softest grass; it almost felt like velvet. She saw tiny little red and white mushrooms and they all had little tiny doors in them. The trees were all different colours; they were beautiful. The flowers were all different shapes and sizes and most of all they were the most amazing colours Amy had ever seen.

In the middle of the grass sat a tiny mushroom with six tiny chairs around it with tiny acorn shells for cups. Rose petals were all over the grass. Amy turned to Cherry and asked, "Why are there rose petals everywhere?"

Cherry looked at Amy and replied, "Every time you see rose petals on the ground, a fairy has just got married. We had a wedding last night. It was fantastic; she looked gorgeous. I wish you could have seen it."

Amy had so many questions that she wanted to ask, like, "What is the mushroom table for?"

"That's when the Queen fairy calls for her meeting. Only six people can go at a time. We sit around the table and she reads to us from the Big Book," Cherry said.

"What's the Big Book?"

"You'll learn about that later. Come on, hurry up," said Cherry.

As the two of them walked along the grassy path, a little pixie called Fern came out from behind a tree.

Fern

"Who's this, Cherry?" Fern asked.

"This is Amy, my new friend. She followed me through the Magical Gate."

Fern gasped. "You mean she's the one?"

"Sssshhh!" said Cherry. "She doesn't know why she is here yet."

"Well, I think it's time for her to know, don't you?" Fern said sternly.

"Okay, Fern, let's tell her."

"Tell me what?" Amy asked.

Cherry began to explain. "Well, you see, Amy, it wasn't a mistake that you came to Fairyland. We need your help. Our big Fairy Book, which tells us everything, is our main source of guidance; it's our life. Remember I told you about how the Queen reads the Book to us? Well, it told us that you are the one."

"The one for what?" asked Amy.

"To help us, silly."

"There must be a mistake. The Book must be wrong. I am only nine years old; how can I possibly help you? And what am I supposed to help you with?" By this time Amy was starting to get very worried.

"No, the Book is never wrong, Amy! Let me show you. You see how beautiful it is here, how the colours are much brighter? Well, that's because no human has ever been here before. Your world and ours are so different. Humans hurt and destroy things. We are frightened of your world."

"But I am a human, and I am here, and I don't hurt or destroy things."

"That's why you are here, and that's why we need you. We need a pure heart, the heart of a child, to destroy the evil goblin and his gang. You see, Shadow hates love and kindness. He hates colour too. Shadow wants to destroy Fairyland and trap all who live in it in your world. He has already taken Marigold and has put her somewhere, we think, in your world. That's why we need you! Our Book told us only the pure heart of a child can defeat his wicked evil ways. Please will you help us?"

"But how am I to destroy Shadow? I'm only a child!" said Amy.

"You still don't understand the power of a child's pure heart, do you? Let me take you to our Queen. She will tell you everything."

Shadow

As they walked they came to a beautiful fairy castle made out of crystal and diamonds that all sparkled in the sunlight.

"This is where our Queen lives. Her name is Diamond."

As they walked inside the castle, Amy noticed that the floor was made from solid gold and there were mirrors all around the corridors. Right at the bottom of the corridor there were two double doors made from pearl. Amy's heart began to race, this time with fear.

"Do not be afraid," Cherry said. "Our Queen is lovely and kind. She will be glad you are here." Cherry's tiny hand banged on the door.

"Come in," Diamond said.

"Your Majesty, I would like you to meet Amy."

"Greetings. I know why you are here," said Diamond.

"You do? I mean, you *know* why I'm here?" Amy said in a puzzled voice.

Cherry said to her Queen, "You see, Amy doesn't understand why she has been brought here. I've told her everything. I thought you could help."

As Diamond stepped down, her beauty unfolded. Her dress was made from silk with tiny diamonds all over it and she had a tiny diamond crown on her head and little emerald shoes.

"Come with me; let me show you your power," Diamond told Amy.

"My power?" asked Amy.

As they walked down the corridor they came to a set of stairs that led to another pearl door. Diamond opened the door. In the middle of the room was a beautifully bound little white Book sitting open on a gold stand. Diamond opened the Book and said, "Amy, come closer." As Amy bent down and moved closer to see this intriguing little Book, Diamond explained that Shadow used to be a part of Fairyland. "He used to be such a wonderful pixie."

"Pixie?" said Amy. "I thought Shadow was a goblin; that's what Cherry told me anyway."

"That's correct, he is, but he used to be a very beautiful pixie," said Cherry. "He is now the most evil goblin you will ever meet."

Diamond went on to explain. "You see, Amy, he was a wonderful pixie; so helpful and kind but he wanted one thing that turned his heart black."

"What was that?" Amy said, inquisitively.

"ULTIMATE POWER," said Diamond. "He wanted to be like me and rule over Fairyland. As he tried to turn all the fairies and pixies against me, he became more and more evil. I had to banish him. Shadow took a third of the pixies with him. They wanted what he had promised them, that they would rule over Fairyland. He promised to destroy this world, and us. Slowly his wickedness started to change his appearance as well. So he turned into an ugly goblin and the rest of the pixies turned into trolls. So, Amy, now you know why we need your help. As a child grows to become a young adult, their heart becomes hard and they stop believing in us. This is why we need you, as your heart is still pure. You've not stopped believing in us. It's only a pure heart of a child that will defeat Shadow."

It all became very clear to Amy that she must help them. She looked at the Queen and said, "Okay. I will help."

"GREAT!" said Diamond.

"Great. I knew you would!" said Cherry.

"Now it's nearly sunset. We will meet in the morning, so watch for the Gate."

Diamond asked Amy to come even closer, and as Amy did, she kissed her on her forehead, saying, "Thank you."

"You're welcome, your Majesty," said Amy, wondering if she had really done the right thing.

As Cherry walked Amy back to the Gate she handed Amy a little purse, inside which was pixie dust.

"You must only use this when you think it's important. It will get you out of trouble."

Amy took the purse. "Thank you, I will look after this."

"I know you will," said Cherry.

Amy looked back and waved. "See you tomorrow," Cherry shouted. Amy smiled as she walked back through the Gate.

The next day, Amy raced through the house.

"Slow down, and don't forget to eat your breakfast. It's on the table!"

"Sorry, Mum, haven't got time for breakfast," laughed Amy.

Her mother stood there shaking her head at Amy as she watched her run into the back garden. Amy couldn't wait to see if the Magical Gate was going to appear. As she waited she put her hand into her pocket and felt for the purse. She realised it wasn't there.

"Oh no," she shouted. She ran back into the house and up into her bedroom, and there under her pillow was the tiny red purse. Just in time too, Mum's changing the bed sheets, she said to herself. She grabbed the purse and ran back into the garden. The Gate was already there, but as she stepped through she noticed that the trees looked dull and the flowers were drooping. Amy looked around. What's gone on here, she thought, and where's Cherry?

"CHERRY! WHERE ARE YOU?" Amy shouted. She could see Fern running towards her.

"Ssssshhhh," he said.

"Why? What's going on and where's Cherry?" Amy whispered.

"Hide! You must hide if you are going to help us. I must protect you. Come with me," he said.

Amy started to panic and began to run with Fern. They ran through the forest and came to a hollow tree; she squeezed through the gap, and watched, her heart racing with fear. Fern turned to her and said, "Cherry has been captured; she didn't come home last night after taking you to the Gate. We were very worried about her; we couldn't find her anywhere. We know that Shadow has her, and he's after as many fairies and pixies as he can lay his hands on."

"Oh, Fern, that's terrible. So why are we in here and not looking for Cherry and Marigold?"

Fern turned to Amy and said, "Watch."

As Amy watched, she saw the most ghastly figure that she had ever seen. He was big and green with a spiked collar around his neck, with impish ears, bright yellow teeth, and yellow eyes to match his teeth; he was disgusting. He also had a big claw hand.

Claw

"Who's that? Is that Shadow?" Amy asked.

"No," whispered Fern, "that's Claw the troll. Sshhh, he will hear you."

As they waited patiently for him to go, Amy asked, "Why is he here? What's he looking for?"

"Fairies. He bags them up and takes them back to Shadow's

castle or Shadow's hideout. He has many hideouts. Shadow then takes them into your world and traps them there. That's why it's important we put a stop to this. Otherwise Fairyland is ruined. Shadow has started to take the colour out of Fairyland; look at the trees and flowers. And he won't stop till there is no colour at all."

"Fern, we have to ride down the slide into Fairyland, we need to tell the Queen that Claw has been here," said Amy.

"I know, but it's just too risky. He normally goes soon."

"How do you know he will go soon?"

"He comes here every day at the same time, for the same thing."

Just then they heard a big scream. Amy jumped and banged her head. "Ouch!" she said, rubbing her head better. Fern sternly looked at her. "What? I banged my head. It hurt, I'm sorry. Who was it that screamed?"

Fern turned to Amy and said, "Oh no, that was Blossom. She lives in the blossom trees."

"How do you know it was Blossom?" said Amy.

Fern looked at Amy and shook his head. He knew this was going to be hard, but he had to explain.

"You see, some fairies live out here in the trees and some live in the flowers. In Fairyland the pixies live in the mushrooms, so we are scattered everywhere."

"But how do you know it was her?" Amy asked. "It could have been anyone."

"You see that tree over there?"

"Yes, what about it?"

"Well, that's hers," Fern said frantically.

Blossom

As they looked at the tree, it began to lose its colour—fast. It became grey and dull as if all life had been sucked from it. Amy couldn't believe what she had just seen.

They noticed Claw talking to another troll.

"Come on, we have what we came for, let's go." The earth shook as they walked by.

"Phew! I thought they would never go," said Fern.

"Me neither," said Amy.

They crawled out of their hiding place and took a long look around. They noticed that many more of the trees had lost their colour. Fern began to further explain to Amy that when a fairy is taken from a flower or a tree, the tree will lose its colour.

"And that's your proof, Amy, that it was Blossom. You see, a fairy is the heart of a tree or flower, and a pixie is the heart of the mushroom. The tree becomes sad and slowly dies; that's why it's important to return the fairy before it's too late."

"Come on, let's go. There's no time to lose," Amy said.

They ran to the hole, slid down the slide, and made their way to the Queen's castle. As they approached the castle they were surprised to be met by the Queen.

"I have been waiting for you. What's taken you so long?"

"Your Majesty!" they both shouted.

"Okay, one at a time. What's happened?"

Fern stepped forward and started to explain how Claw had taken Blossom to Shadow's castle.

"We must act now, Your Majesty, we are losing fairies fast. And the colour is leaving the trees and flowers too."

The Queen blew her magical trumpet and all the fairies and pixies flew to her command. Amy was amazed to see so many beautiful fairies in all different colours.

"They're amazing," said Amy.

The Queen stepped forward and said, "Shadow has taken three fairies so far. You must be on your guard, and look out for Shadow's henchmen."

Amy remembered the little red purse that Cherry had given her before she was taken.

"What's this for, Your Majesty? Cherry gave it to me. She told me to use it when it's really important. She said it will get me out of trouble."

"That's correct. It's pixie dust. Sprinkle this on yourself and you will become invisible and able to get out of trouble, but it only lasts a few minutes."

"Where is Shadow's castle, Your Majesty? I want to find my friend," Amy said.

The Queen turned to Amy and said, "It's deep in the heart of the forest where all the toadstools grow, but you must be careful." She looked at Fern and said, "Fern, you must go with Amy as you know the forest well, but be careful."

"Yes, Your Majesty, I will look after Amy. I will guard her as best I can."

The Queen turned again to Amy and said, "You can start your journey in the morning. You must go to the Gate before it disappears. Until tomorrow, take care, Amy, my brave warrior."

"Thank you, Your Majesty, I will," said Amy.

Fern walked Amy back to the Gate. "We must be careful," he said. "Any of Shadow's men can be near the Gate. Stay here."

Amy stayed where she was; she hid behind a tall tree and looked around. I can't see anyone, she thought. She was just about to come out when she heard a voice that sounded familiar.

"Let me go! You're going to pay for this, you all are. HELP ME! Somebody HELP!"

Amy knew that voice; it was Fern's. Amy started to panic as she was all on her own. The Gate was about to appear and she had to tell the Queen about Fern. Amy ran as fast as she could and slid back down the slide just in time.

"HELP ME! HELP ME!" she shouted. "Fern's been captured. I need someone to help."

Amy heard a quiet little voice say, "Amy, I am Lavender. I'll help you. Let's go and tell Diamond. She'll know what to do."

As Amy looked at Lavender she couldn't help but notice just what a pretty fairy she was. She had never seen such beauty in someone so small. She wore a purple dress and had long dark hair, and on her feet she wore little tiny green leaf-shaped shoes.

As they passed the mushroom patch, Amy noticed that one of them had lost its colour. Amy knew that was Fern's house, and a single tear ran down Amy's face. She had felt helpless as she couldn't help Fern get away from the evil troll.

"Don't cry, Amy. You will find all the fairies, and Fern; I know you will."

They came to the Queen's castle and banged on the door. The door slowly began to open.

"That's strange," said Lavender. "That doesn't normally happen."

Amy had a bad feeling about this. Maybe Shadow has her too, but how? she thought.

They both walked inside and found that the Queen was gone.

"Oh no! Diamond's gone too!" said Lavender. She grabbed Amy's hand and ran down the spiral stairs.

"Where are we going?" Amy shouted.

"To where the magical Book is."

"But why? Do you think it's gone too?" Amy just had to know.

"No. I don't know, but I'm sure if it's still here then it will tell us what happened to her. You see, Shadow is called Shadow because when it becomes dark you can't see him. You can only see him in the sunlight, and it's why he comes out night."

As they reached the Book it slowly began to open, and spoke to them.

"Shadow has taken the Queen; he has bagged her up and taken her to the human world. He is guarding her himself. You must take Thorn. He also knows the forest and will know what to do." The Book closed.

Amy looked at Lavender and said, "Who's Thorn?"

"Oh, he's Fern's brother. You'll like him; he will remind you of Fern," said Lavender.

They ran to Thorn's mushroom and knocked on the door. As Thorn opened the door, Amy couldn't believe her eyes. It was just like looking at Fern. "Remarkable," she said.

Thorn looked at them and said, "I know what I have to do. I've been watching what happened."

They walked Amy quietly back to the Gate. Amy ran through it, and looked back as the Gate disappeared.

Thorn

She had got back just in time as her dinner was just being put on the table. After dinner, she went up into her bedroom and got ready for bed. She put the purse back under her pillow and settled down to sleep.

As Amy closed her eyes she began to dream. She could see a dark shadow looming over her. The shadowy figure began to tell her, "Stay away, stay away from Fairyland; they do not need you. If you don't stay away, I will capture you, and you will never see anyone ever again." Amy began to toss and turn and she began to talk in her sleep. "Go away, leave me alone! I will rescue the fairies and you can't stop me." She could see all the fairies being held in a dark, cold place. They were crying and looked so sad. Amy could see Claw and many other nasty trolls and evil beasts; they each had bags of fairies. From the bags she heard screams of, "Help us, Amy, you must help us." Amy woke up, screaming. Her mum came running into her bedroom.

"Amy, what's up? Why are you so upset?"

"Oh, Mum, I've had a terrible dream; lots of fairies being captured and taken to cold, dark places. They were all asking me for help, and evil trolls and beasts had them. Mum, it was horrible!"

Mum began to laugh and said, "Amy darling, it's only a dream, you know fairies don't really exist."

Amy understood now. She knew the Queen was right about grown-ups: their hearts are hard and unbelieving. She knew she had to help them. More now than ever before. Amy smiled at her mum. As her mum settled her back down to sleep, she bent down and kissed her. "Goodnight, honey, sleep tight," said Mum.

"Night, Mum." As her mum closed the door, leaving Amy in the dark, Amy became terrified. She was hoping she would not dream the same dream again. She began to drift off to sleep.

Chapter Two

AMY WOKE UP VERY EARLY and very troubled. Her heart was racing with fear, and her hands began to shake. She thought about Shadow and what he had said to her in her nightmare. The dream was so fresh Amy could still hear the fairies shouting, over and over again, saying, "Amy, we need you, we need your help, please help us."

Amy froze to the spot in fear and thought to herself, no, I can do this, I have to.

Just then, as if by magic, she heard Diamond's voice say, "Amy, it's the pure heart, a heart of a child, who can defeat Shadow." Amy wondered where that voice had come from. She sat up straight and said, "Who else is going to help them? Cherry is my friend; she needs me. Let's do this." Amy felt so much stronger.

She found her backpack underneath her bed. She looked around her bedroom for things she might need for her journey but couldn't think of anything, so she decided to look in the kitchen. She grabbed her backpack and made her way into the kitchen. She began making herself a ham sandwich. She packed a torch and an apple. Might need some string too, she thought, it could act as a rope for them, as they are very small.

Amy looked around the kitchen and said to herself, "Let's go. I am ready for battle." She walked out of her back door that led into the garden; she got on her bike and put her backpack into her basket. "I can get there faster and Thorn can ride in the basket," she said.

The Gate appeared and Amy rode her bike through it. Amy stared around her. The whole forest had completely lost its colour; it looked terribly dull and unattractive.

Oh no! I'm too late, thought Amy.

Thorn met her by the hole; he had a very worried look on his face. Oh no, thought Amy again, I don't want to hear this.

"I am afraid I have more bad news—all the tree fairies from this part of Fairyland have been captured. They were playing late last night. Claw and Bones got them. I could hear them screaming and calling for you, Amy."

Amy became very frightened as she realised that her dream had been real. She began to tell Thorn all about it and what Shadow had said to her. Thorn went very pale, and turned to her and said, "Shadow appears to people in dreams; he's the one responsible for children's nightmares."

"Oh no, you mean to tell me that my dream was real? We must hurry." Amy bent down to pick Thorn up. She carefully placed him in her basket. "There you go, nice and safe," she said.

"No, you must leave your bike here; it's too risky, we need to be quiet. You see all the trees that have lost their colour? Well, Shadow has made them into spies. They have to let him know when anybody comes or he will completely destroy them."

"Okay," said Amy.

Amy noticed that the forest was looking spooky. It was rather frightening—there were dark toadstools everywhere and all the sounds were weird. There was no bird song, no bees buzzing; all the friendly sounds had gone, and had been replaced by scary sounds.

"What's happened, Thorn? The forest is frightening me."

Thorn stared at Amy and said, "That's what Shadow wants. He wants to put fear into us. That way we will obey him. Look closer at the trees."

Amy looked around and stared at the trees. She noticed that they all had faces, and their branches were their arms.

"Be careful. Don't wake them up; they all work for Shadow now. They will let him know we are here," said Thorn. "We must go quietly or they will try and capture us."

As they walked slowly through the forest, Amy's heart began to race faster than she had ever known before. She was hoping not to alert any of the trees. Just then the earth began to shake. Amy looked at Thorn. "What was that?"

Thorn put his tiny hand over her mouth. He began to whisper, "Shhhhh, don't say another word. Stay there."

Amy began to feel sick. Her heart was pounding. She was sure the trees would hear it pounding; she knew they could. As Thorn flew higher he could see who was making all the noise; it was Bones. Thorn knew they were in great danger, and they should get out of there as soon as possible. He flew back to Amy and said, "We must get out of here and hide; it's Bones, one of Shadow's henchmen."

They looked around for somewhere to hide, but where were they going to hide? The trees worked for Shadow now. All except for one; the little willow tree.

"Pssst," said the little tree. "You can hide in my flowing branches and leaves. I am not on Shadow's side. I just miss my friend, Willow. I want to help you as I know that's what Willow would have wanted me to do."

They quietly tiptoed over to the willow tree and went into its leaves as it folded its branches over them. They began to watch, peering out from within the branches. As the ground pounded, so did Amy's heart. She saw the most ghastly sight that she had ever seen. He was huge and green with a big wart on the end of his nose. Around his neck he wore a bone necklace. He had big red eyes. I suppose that's why they call him Bones, Amy thought to herself.

She heard him say in a big loud gruff voice, "Has anyone been around here yet? Anyone like a little girl?" Amy knew that he was talking about her. Her heart began to pound louder. Be quiet, heart, she thought, please be quiet. The trees all shook their branches and said in echoing voices, "No, Bones, we would tell you if we saw anyone."

"Make sure you do or I'll rip you out of the ground and you'll die forever." As he went, he looked at the willow tree and said, "And that goes for you too." The tree never said a word.

"Phew! I thought he had seen us," said Thorn.

"We must get out of here," Amy said.

The tree opened up his branches, and they tiptoed out into the forest and made their way back to the Magical Gate. Amy looked at Thorn and said, "Why are we here? I thought we had to go to Shadow's castle?"

"No, we ought not to be here. We have to find the other fairies and put them back into their tree; it's not safe with the trees on Shadow's side. As soon as we put the tree fairies back, their colour will return, and then they will be on our side again. The willow tree had a lucky escape with his branches that flowed over him. His leaves hid him a little," said Thorn.

Amy made her way back through the Magical Gate and sat on her grass. One thing puzzled her. Where was she to start looking for her friends? Just then her eyes fell on a hole underneath her garden shed. She quickly got up, ran over and bent down to have a closer look at the hole. She thought, I am too big to fit down there. She wondered how she was ever going to fit in that hole. She called quietly for Thorn. And told him about the hole.

"I am sure one of the fairies is in there but I am too big to fit," Amy said in a panic.

"Okay, I'll take a look for you, but what makes you think one of them is in there? Surely the hole would be much bigger for one of the trolls to fit in," said Thorn.

"I have never noticed that hole before," said Amy. "And my dream is still fresh in my mind. I saw one of them, or even all of them, in a dark, cold place. It's worth a look, Thorn,"

Thorn flew down the hole, which led into a long corridor. This is too easy, thought Thorn. But the corridor went on and on and on. Thorn was getting worried and decided to turn back and head for Amy.

As he flew back he heard a really scary sound of growling and grunting. Thorn's heart began to pound. Thorn frantically looked for somewhere to hide, but there was nowhere to turn, nowhere to hide. Then Thorn remembered the pixie dust. He took some out of his pocket and quickly sprinkled some on himself, and as he did, he disappeared.

Thorn decided to stay where he was just to see what all the grunting was about. To his amazement he saw Bones and Claw coming down the corridor. How had they fitted down that hole, thought Thorn? Then he remembered Amy. Had they captured her too? Thorn started to panic and flew back up the hole. As the daylight hit Thorn he reappeared. Thorn sighed a sigh of relief to see Amy waiting at the same place that he had left her. Thorn was amazed, and frantically asked Amy if she had seen the two trolls, or was there another way for them to get in?

"No, I've seen no one, I've been here the whole time."

"Calm down, Amy. I think you could be right," said Thorn. "There was a long corridor that went on for a long time. I decided to turn back at that point. That's when I heard the trolls. So I put the pixie dust on myself. I stayed there for a while and to my amazement I saw Bones and Claw. What I would like to know is how they got down such a tiny hole. We have to find out! And you must get some rest. You are no good to us while you are so upset. And your mother will be looking for you soon. We will carry on looking in the morning. In the meantime I will try and find out how they got down that hole,"

"No, Thorn, I am fine," said Amy. "We need to keep looking. I am only a little late; that's not a problem."

"Amy, please go home. Let me find out what I can, and how they got down there. I'll tell you in the morning. We will meet by the Magical Gate bright and early," Thorn said.

"Okay, I will see you then." Amy smiled and walked back to her house. Before she went in she turned around and waved at Thorn.

Meanwhile back in Fairyland, Thorn made his way to his house. He knew he had a book of spells in the drawer. Maybe this would tell him how they got down that tiny hole. He opened the door and went in. He walked over to the drawer and pulled out a big book, and as he opened it, he searched the pages for any clues. All of a sudden, he came across something interesting—shrinking dust.

"Shrinking dust—what's that?" Thorn said. Then the book began to talk and said, "Well, Thorn, it's a powder that makes you shrink; it helps you to get into small gaps."

Thorn jumped back and dropped the book onto the floor as he was not expecting the book to talk to him. "THAT'S IT!" he shouted. "That's how they did it." He turned to the book and said, "How can I get some?"

The book began to talk and said, "Pick me up." Thorn bent down and picked the book up. He turned the pages. The book said, "You will see a list of the ingredients. You must collect them all and make the potion and take it on your journey." At that point, the book began to close.

"Wait! Where do I collect them from?" shouted Thorn, frantically.

The book said, faintly, "Around Fairyland."

As Thorn walked outside, he held the page he had torn out from the book in his hand. It read: "One spotty mushroom… ". Thorn knew where they were, but as he went over to the mushroom patch he noticed that there was only one left. That's strange, thought Thorn. I was sure there were more here than that.

As he bent down to pick one, he noticed a big footprint that only a troll could have made. Thorn gasped as he knew he was running out of time. He read on. It said, "One spotty mushroom, one rose petal, two almond seeds, and one parsley leaf. Mix them in boiling water for twenty minutes. Pour into a little bottle."

As Thorn mixed them all together he knew the trolls would be back for more of the potion. He poured the last little drop into a bottle. He decided it was time to get some rest as he had a big day in the morning. He carefully opened his door and placed the bottle on his kitchen table. Hopefully, Amy would have calmed down by then, he thought to himself.

Thorn got up bright and early and put the shrinking potion in his knapsack; he also packed a tiny torch. Thorn put his shoes on, which were made out of little leaves, and his cap, which was made from an acorn shell. His clothes were made from pure silk; he had a white silk shirt and a green silk leaf shape waistcoat and green tights. Over the top of the tights he wore green shorts.

"Okay, now I am ready to go and find my friends, and defeat Claw," said Thorn. He looked out of his window just to make sure it was safe as he knew that any of Shadow's henchmen could be outside after more ingredients to make the potion.

"Okay, all safe," said Thorn. He opened his door and made his way to the Magical Gate where he waited for Amy. As Amy appeared Thorn told her about the shrinking potion that he had made.

"So that's how they got in," said Amy.

"We have to hurry. Come on!" Thorn shouted.

As they both approached the hole, Thorn took out the potion and carefully sprinkled some onto Amy to make her fit through the hole. Amy slowly began to shrink.

Amy suddenly felt very frightened and vulnerable and a little strange but she knew she had to follow Thorn. She wondered what was down there. What lay in wait for her at the other end of the tunnel? Oh well, only one way to find out, thought Amy. She looked at Thorn and said, "We are the same size now. Come on, let's go."

Thorn looked at Amy and said, "You wait here. Let me first go down and make sure it's safe for us."

"Okay," Amy said.

Thorn flew down and thought it was perfectly safe for Amy to follow. But something didn't seem quite right; it was too quiet. Thorn knew they had to take things very carefully as they could be walking straight into a trap. Thorn flew up to Amy and told her that they must be very careful as it was too quiet for his liking. The two tiny friends held each other's hands. Thorn looked at Amy and said, "We must stay together."

"Okay, I understand," said Amy.

Thorn flew down the hole with Amy hanging on tightly. As they both reached the bottom, Amy looked at Thorn and said, "I see what you mean; it's too quiet down here." As they both started to walk down the long corridor, Amy noticed that it seemed to go on forever. Amy's heart began to race with fear. What would they meet around the next corner? Amy was too scared to find out, but knew she had no choice.

Chapter Three

AS THEY CREPT AROUND THE next corner they heard the frightening sounds of growling and thumping in amongst the quietness. They stopped in their tracks. Thorn said, "Stay there while I take a closer look." Amy was only too pleased to stay where she was. It all sounded really scary. As Thorn peered around the corner, he saw Bones mixing up something and he could see Cherry being held captive. But what was Bones doing? He needed to get a closer look, but how? He flew back to Amy and said, "I've seen Cherry, but Bones has her. He's mixing something up in a big black pot. I need to get a closer look, so I would need to use the invisible potion. I should be able to get close enough to be able to see what he is doing."

As Bones stood around the big black pot he had a big red and gold book that he was reading from.

"Okay, if I put half of a rotten cabbage in and then one dog's eye … mustn't forget the cat's liver and the special ingredient is fairy dust. I must have this." He grabbed Cherry and bellowed, "Where is the fairy dust? I must have this to make my sleeping potion."

Cherry gazed at Bones and laughed, "If you think I am telling you where the fairy dust is, you must be mad. NEVER! I tell you, NEVER!"

This only made Bones even madder, and he grabbed Cherry's cage and hung it over the black pot and said to her, "This is where you will be until you tell me where the fairy dust is. Enjoy the heat, little fairy. No one will save you, or can even hear you. You will be the next ingredient in the pot if you don't tell me what I need to know. I must tell you that by your every move you will lower the cage further into the pot, ha ha ha ha."

Bones put the cage over the black pot and stuffed Cherry into it, closed and locked the door. As Cherry watched Bones walk away she was struck by fear. She began to shake, and as she shook, the cage began to slowly lower. Cherry knew she had to keep calm and very still, but how was she to stay so still? She was so frightened; her tiny heart was racing. All kinds of thoughts were going through Cherry's mind. Would Amy ever rescue her? Or would she actually be the next ingredient?

Cherry had to think positive. She looked down. She could see the pot bubbling away and the heat was getting hotter and hotter. The sweat began to drip from Cherry's brow. She knew that time was running out for her. She began to feel faint as the heat reached her, sucking away her oxygen.

Cherry felt a single tear run down her face. As she slowly closed her eyes, she began to think of Fern and Amy, not realising that Fern had been captured too. She knew in her heart that they would rescue her if they could; they would never let her down. As Thorn looked on he began to panic as he could see Cherry lying at the bottom of the cage as if dead. He knew he had to get Amy quickly.

Thorn flew back to Amy and said, "I need to drink the magic potion now."

"Okay, but why?" shouted Amy.

"I can see Cherry." Thorn began drink the magic potion, and as he drank so he turned invisible. Thorn thought this was great as he could see Amy, but she could no longer see him. Amy looked around and began to whisper, "Thorn, are you still here?"

"Of course I am. I'll be able to get really close like this. Just hope it doesn't wear off too quickly, or I might be in trouble before I can rescue Cherry."

Thorn flew up to the cage and tried to open the door, but the door was locked. He panicked. How was he going to get this door open? As he tugged on the door, the cage slowly lowered into the boiling mixture! He now knew he had an even bigger problem. Not only was the door locked, but the cage was moving down, heading towards the green bubbling slime. In all seriousness he knew time was running out.

Thorn shouted, "CHERRY? CHERRY? Can you hear me? You need to wake up. CHERRY?"

Thorn took one last look around in case Bones had put the key somewhere. As he looked and looked, he was just about to give up in despair when a shiny object in the corner of the room caught his eye. Thorn saw what looked like a large key on a hook, just to the side of a shelf. His heart jumped for joy in the hope that he had finally found the key to the cage. Thorn flew up towards the key and tried with all his might to lift the key off the hook. His heart began to sink as he knew he wasn't strong enough. He looked back at Cherry who was just lying there, looking lifeless. Thorn shouted to Cherry in desperation.

"I won't be long. Hang in there, I am going to get Amy. We'll get you out. I have seen a key."

Thorn flew faster than ever. He flew so fast he nearly flew past Amy.

"Thorn!" shouted Amy. She knew something was wrong before Thorn had even told her. "What's happened? Is Cherry okay? I need to know."

"No time to waste, Amy. Drink some invisible potion and follow me. You need to hurry."

Amy began to drink really fast and she felt kind of strange; all shivery with pins and needles in her legs. As she looked down at her feet they started to disappear, then her legs and body, till there was nothing left to see. Amy felt a little scared but also very excited.

Thorn shouted, "FOLLOW ME, QUICKLY!" Amy ran as fast

as she could; her heart was racing with fear. She needed to stop to catch her breath, but she knew if she stopped she would lose Thorn as he was flying much too fast for her. But why? Amy thought. What has happened?

Finally, Thorn stopped flying and had come to a cave-like room. The light was dim; it was really hard to see. Thorn turned to Amy and pointed at the cage hanging over the pot. As Amy's eyes focused she could see Cherry lying still on the cage floor. Amy began to panic and feared the worst.

"We need to get her out of there, Thorn."

Thorn nodded and pointed to the key on the hook.

"We need to get this key down, Amy, and it's too heavy for me on my own. I think the key will unlock the cage door. We must hurry, though. I hope she is still alive. I don't know how long Cherry can hold out or how long we have till Bones comes back."

Amy nodded and grabbed tightly onto Thorn's hand. "Let's fly," she said.

Thorn took off and flew Amy over to where the key was. They landed on the corner of the shelf with the key just below them.

"We will have to work together; this key is far too heavy for me alone," said Thorn.

Amy and Thorn bent down and took hold of the key together. "Don't drop it, Amy. We will lift on three. One, two, three, lift!"

To Thorn's amazement, Amy was stronger than she looked. Amy said, "Thorn, I think I can lift this key on my own. Let me try and open the cage door."

"I must warn you, Amy; be very careful as you open the cage. As the cage moves so it also lowers into the pot. If the cage moves any more, she's fairy food."

Amy grabbed the key and nervously walked along the shelf to where the cage hung over the pot, hoping all the while that she would not send Cherry plummeting. Her heart was thumping and she was sure she could hear it this time.

Amy picked the key up and reached up to the cage to try it in the lock. She noticed that the green slimy mixture in the pot was moving, then it stopped, and then moved. Amy didn't know what this was, and didn't want to know either. She knew she had to hurry as Bones was coming back. The key felt slippery in Amy's hands as they began to sweat. Keep calm, she thought. The key slowly went into the lock; she turned it and opened the door. Her hand reached into the cage and gently pulled out Cherry. As Amy brought Cherry out, her hand hit the cage. The cage went crashing down into the pot; and was instantly sucked into the mixture. Amy breathed a sigh of relief, as she was looking at Cherry lying in her arms.

Thorn walked over to them and said, "Look! She's turning invisible too!" Amy was amazed as she looked at her. Now they could all go unseen. Thorn knew they had to get out of there as they could now hear footsteps thumping closer and closer.

"Let's go," said Thorn. Amy ran as fast as she could. Even though she knew that Bones couldn't see her, she wanted to be as far away from him as she possibly could. Thorn grabbed Amy's arm and said, "No, wait! He can't see us. Let's see what he's up to."

They stood there as Bones came thumping past the three of them. Amy put her hand over her nose and screwed up her face.

"What's that awful smell, Thorn?"

Thorn laughed and said, "That's Bones. They all smell horrible, just like him."

Amy felt sick; it smelt like a slimy rotten cabbage with a hint of wet dog. As the two watched, they discovered that he was indeed making some sort of potion. Bones picked up a big wooden spoon and pulled the cage out of the pot; he began to laugh.

"I've done it. I've created sleeping gas with the last ingredient which was that stupid fairy. Now I can put all the fairies to sleep in Fairyland."

He began to pour the mixture into several glass jars and stored them right on the top shelf. Thorn laughed and said, "Let's get out of here."

As the two friends walked out into the fresh air, the potions wore off and they returned to normal. Amy looked at Cherry but she still wasn't moving. Instead she looked lifeless.

"I know what she needs," shouted Amy. She began to run to the acorn tree which was at the bottom of her garden. She found a tiny acorn shell on the ground and picked it up, walked over to her mum's bird fountain, and put the shell into the water and filled the cup up. She laid Cherry on her lap and held her head half up. She put the shell up to Cherry's lips. As the water touched Cherry's mouth she began to open her eyes. Things were a bit blurred for Cherry until her eyes focused. She was so pleased to see Thorn and especially pleased to see Amy. As Cherry sat up she had one question for the two of them

"Where's Fern?"

Amy looked at Thorn and thought it was best for him to tell her. Thorn looked at Cherry and sadly said, "Fern was captured along with the other tree fairies. And I was told to take over."

Cherry sat in silence for a moment. Thorn and Amy noticed that the corner of Cherry's wing had been torn. "DON'T MOVE!" they both shouted.

Cherry sat very still, wondering what was behind her, and why she had to sit so still. Amy laughed and quietly said, "Don't be afraid; nothing will hurt you now, but I can see you've hurt your wing, that's all." Amy began to put a tiny stick onto her wing, and picked a blade of grass and tied the stick in place

"That will take time to mend," Thorn whispered. Amy looked at Cherry; she looked so fragile, nothing like she did when they first met.

"She will need a safe place to stay," Thorn said. "We can't take her back to Fairyland; it's not safe. As soon as she arrives in Fairyland, her tree will blossom again, and Bones thinks she's fallen into the pot. He will know for sure she has survived. We must think of somewhere else she could stay."

Amy knew she had to do something for her friend while she was recovering. Suddenly she had a wonderful idea.

"I know where she can stay. She can stay in my bedroom. I can make her a little bed, and it will only be until she has completely recovered," she said. Amy could see by the look on Thorn's face that he did not like that idea. "What's not to like, Thorn? She'll be safe away from Shadow and Bones and Claw. You've said yourself it will take a while for her wing to mend. My bedroom is safe. My Mum only comes in to make my bed, but if I make my own bed she won't even come in. She'll be safe. I can make her a bed in my trinket box or, better still, in my doll's house. She'll love it; no one looks in there. Oh please, Thorn, what do you say? Oh please say yes. Please?"

Amy looked at Thorn with eyes wide open, awaiting his answer. Thorn turned to Amy and said, "I don't know. I don't have a good feeling about this. The human world is so different than ours; so much can go wrong. We are frightened of your world."

For the very first time Amy could see fear in Thorn's eyes. Thorn turned to Cherry and asked her what she thought.

"Thorn, I'd like that after what I've been through. That's the only safe place I know at the moment. I feel safe around Amy," Cherry answered.

"Okay then, but only if you are sure, Cherry," Thorn answered.

Cherry looked at Thorn. "I am sure," she said.

"Well, I'd better hurry as the Magical Gate has just appeared. I must go through it. Please, Amy, take care of her," Thorn said, worriedly.

"Don't worry, she'll be fine. Now go. I'll meet you back here at the hole tomorrow at the same time," whispered Amy.

Thorn turned to look at Cherry who was now sitting in Amy's hand. "Stay safe. I'll see you in the morning," he gently told her.

Cherry took hold of Thorn's hand and whispered, "No, you stay safe. Watch out for Shadow; he could be anywhere."

Cherry felt very sad. This was going to be the first time since her capture that she had ever been away from Fairyland and Thorn. She felt very scared as she was about to go inside Amy's house. She had heard of so many bad stories of what can happen to fairies in the human world. She knew she had to be brave for her own sake and Thorn's. She watched Thorn fly through the Magical Gate. Her heart felt heavy and sad. She whispered, "Hurry back soon, Thorn."

Amy looked at Cherry and noticed that she was crying. "It will be okay, Cherry, he'll be back for you in no time at all."

Cherry wiped her tears, smiled, and gently said in a quivering voice, "I know he will."

Amy put Cherry carefully in her backpack and walked back to her house. Cherry could feel her heart racing. She was sure Amy could hear it. All she knew was that Amy had agreed to look after her. She kept saying over and over again, "I will be safe. I will be safe."

As Amy gently put her backpack onto her bed she started to unzip the bag and carefully took Cherry out. Cherry sat in Amy's hand and took a good look around her bedroom.

"Wow! This is really big, and it's so warm in here."

Amy sat on her bedroom floor in front of her doll's house and said, "Cherry, this will be your house. The furniture is your size; you will be safe in here. You have windows to look out of too. You'll love it." Amy carefully kissed Cherry's tiny head and gently put her down in the house. "Get some rest now," she said.

Chapter Four

A s CHERRY WALKED OVER TO the tiny little bed she began to calm down. She felt so safe in this house knowing that Amy was only inches away from her. Cherry sat down on the bed and felt extremely tired; she'd had a very long and hard day. As she closed her eyes she drifted into a deep sleep and started to dream about Bones holding her over the pot. She could feel Bones pulling and tugging at her wings, demanding that she tell him where the fairy dust was kept. Cherry began to toss and turn in her sleep; she began shouting, "NEVER! NEVER!"

Amy soon realised something was wrong. She opened the doll's house door and gently said, "Cherry, wake up, it's only a dream. Don't worry, I am here. No one can hurt you now." Amy reached into the doll's house and carefully picked her up. She could see by the look on Cherry's face that she was frightened. Amy had never seen anyone look as afraid as Cherry was.

"What happened to you, Cherry? What did they do to you?"

Cherry looked up and smiled a sweet little smile, and said, "You really want to know?"

"Yes, I do."

Cherry walked over and sat on a comfy beanbag. She looked so lost on it as she fell into the middle of the bag. Amy began to laugh. "Oh, Cherry, you are funny. Let me sit you on my pillow." Amy carefully picked her up so as not to hurt her wing and placed her onto her bed. "Okay, Cherry, now you can tell me what happened to you. It must have been horrible for you, but you're safe now."

Cherry cleared her throat and began to tell her story. "Well," she said. "It all began when I left you at the Gate. As I was coming home I was watching the tree fairies play in the warm breeze; they looked so happy. Blossom and Corn were having so much fun with the bees. So I sat down on the grass. I didn't think it would hurt, but then all of a sudden it went pitch black. I couldn't see anything for a while. My eyes focused and when they did I was in this big smelly sack, and soon after, Corn and Blossom joined me. We could hear Bones laughing; we all huddled together, and then before we knew what was happening, Oakie and Willow were thrown into the sack too.

"It was horrible, Amy, we were so frightened! Bones must have walked for miles; well, that's what it seemed like. We didn't know what to expect. Were we going to be fairy food? When we arrived, we had so many things whirling round our minds. We all decided that whatever happened to us, we would never tell any of them any Fairyland secrets, or where anything was, especially the Queen's Big Book. That's our life in that Book; if the trolls got their hands on that, then Fairyland would be no more. And that would be completely dreadful. We really have to stop them, Amy!"

Amy tried to calm Cherry down, but Cherry wanted to fix the problem now. "We must find Willow and Corn, and not forgetting one of my best friends, Blossom."

Cherry began to cry. Amy looked at her; she felt so helpless. It was the middle of the night, and if her mother found out that she had snuck out she would be in so much trouble. But what could she do? She couldn't let Cherry cry and think she wasn't interested in helping her because that wasn't true.

Suddenly she had a great idea, and she shouted, "DO YOU KNOW A SPELL TO SLOW DOWN TIME?"

Cherry jumped up and said, "Why, yes, I do! In fact, that's

one of my favourite spells."

Cherry stood up; she felt about six feet tall. She felt brave and victorious as she started to mutter, "Slow down time, the hands on the clock must stand still." All of a sudden, Amy felt the ground begin to shake. And as she looked at the clock she noticed the hands weren't moving. Time certainly had stood still.

"It is done."

Amy had all sorts of emotions running around her body: some fear, some excitement. She began to get dressed and found her blue jeans and a nice warm jumper. She turned to Cherry, smiled and gently said, "Dress warmly; it will be cold out tonight." Amy found a tiny doll's jumper for Cherry, hoping that it wouldn't be too big for her. She carefully placed the jumper over Cherry's head, but as she carefully folded her wings in, her face was squinting with pain. Amy found some scissors and carefully cut two tiny holes in the jumper for her wings to fit through. It fitted perfectly. Amy was so pleased it worked. Next were the tiny socks she placed on Cherry's tiny feet, and slipped her fairy slippers back on. She looked good; really good.

"Okay, let's go, Cherry." Amy grabbed her bag and coat on the way out, and carefully placed Cherry into her pocket. She closed her bedroom door; she could hear her dad snoring really loudly. Cherry looked at Amy and whispered, "What's that noise?"

Amy giggled very quietly and said, "It's only my dad. He always snores when he's asleep."

Amy tiptoed very quietly past her parents' bedroom door so as not to wake them up. Her heart was racing and her palms began to sweat; she started to feel sick again. Once she was past their door she felt much better. She slid down the banister to avoid the creaky stair. Once she was downstairs she began to relax a little. She found the back door key, which Mum always put on the kitchen counter behind the microwave. She placed the key quietly in the lock and slowly turned the key. The door opened. She took the key out and closed the door. Mustn't forget to lock it, she thought. She locked the door and placed the key in her backpack.

Amy couldn't believe she had done it; she had gotten out of the house without her mum knowing. This is great, she thought. Dangerous, but great. She placed her hand into her pocket and took Cherry out. She held Cherry up to her face and said, "We'd better find Thorn, but how can we get into Fairyland without the Gate appearing. It only appears in the daytime?"

Cherry laughed and said, "I am a fairy, aren't I?"

Amy hung her head in shame. "Oooops, sorry."

Cherry stood up and chanted the words, "Gate closed. Gate appear. Open and make your special glow and come alive." Just as she said this, the Gate appeared and began to glow. Amy was so excited she kissed Cherry on her tiny head, placed her back into her pocket and walked through the Gate.

"You'd better stay in my pocket or your tree will blossom."

As she walked through the Gate, her heart was pounding. She could feel that something was wrong. She looked towards the Fairy hole, and it was surrounded by tiny spikes. Amy did not like the look of this. She found a large hole in a tree, carefully crawled inside, and began to tell Cherry about the spikes around the hole. Cherry peered out of her pocket and saw them.

"What are they? What are those tiny spikes, and how are we going to get Thorn now the hole is guarded?" Amy asked.

Cherry carefully looked at the spikes. She placed her hand over her mouth and gasped.

"They are the spiked guards of Shadow; they are like snails, but faster. They have one downfall: leaves and acorns. They love them. We need to collect acorns or leaves, and throw them far away from the hole, and then you can see how fast they travel."

Amy looked at Cherry and said, "You can't come! You must stay here; we mustn't let your tree know you're back." Amy gently put Cherry into her backpack and placed it onto the ground. She cautiously crept out of the tree, and looked around in case the trees were watching her. And to her surprise they were fast asleep. Great, she thought, and she carefully walked over to where the acorns were and began to gather loads of them, stuffing them into her pockets. She headed back over to the hollow tree to collect her bag. Cherry looked at Amy and said, "Okay, I will count to five, and on five you must run behind those trees. Are you ready?"

Amy carefully placed her bag onto her back. "READY!" she shouted.

"Five. NOW!"said Cherry.

Amy ran out as fast as she could. She threw the acorns past the Fairy hole. They hurled through the air past the spiky snails. The snails moved so fast Amy could hardly believe her eyes. "Did you see that!" she shouted.

"Let's go."

Amy ran for the hole; she just made it in time. She slid down the slide and once again was in Fairyland. Amy looked around for Thorn's house but, to her surprise, it was also surrounded by spiky snails.

"Oh no, not more snails. How could they have got here?" As Cherry peeked out of Amy's bag she could see the snails and even more around the Queen's castle. Cherry had hoped that no one had given Shadow or Bones any of the secrets to Fairyland, let alone the Book. Cherry looked up and told Amy to throw more acorns. As Amy threw the acorns the snails moved like lightning; it was incredible. She ran over to Thorn's house and banged frantically on the door.

"Thorn, open the door! It's Amy and Cherry, let us in quick!" The door flew open and Amy was pulled inside. No sooner did the door shut than the snails were back, guarding it.

"I am so pleased you guys are okay," said Thorn. "I've been so worried about you. It's not safe here; we have to go somewhere to talk. I have so much to tell you."

"Get into my pocket, Thorn."

As soon as he'd climbed onto Amy's hand she placed him into her pocket. Amy took Cherry out of her bag and placed her onto her hand. Cherry stood tall, and once again began to chant.

"Somewhere to hide, somewhere safe, take us out by the Gate."

As quick as they could blink, they were standing by the Magical Gate. They crawled into the hollow tree. Amy took Thorn out from her pocket and placed him onto the leafy ground. Cherry had so many questions as to why the spiky snails were there. Thorn began to tell them how Bones had found out that Cherry had escaped.

"But how?" asked Amy.

"Bones came to Fairyland with what he thought was sleeping gas. I heard he tried to make the fairies sleep. Once he had found out that it hadn't worked he knew she had escaped. When he returned without her, Shadow commanded the snails to guard Fairyland and my home, waiting for her to return."

"How do you know this, Thorn?" Amy asked nervously.

"I heard the trolls talking on my way home from yours last night; they were laughing and making fun of Bones. You can imagine how angry he is with you, Cherry. I heard he wants revenge. I must admit I found it funny; I would have loved to have seen his face when nothing happened. Not one single fairy fell asleep; how funny is that? So I made a spell to go home without a sound. There I stayed until you two came."

Cherry began to giggle. Amy was very confused.

"How did Shadow know?" Amy inquired.

"Well, Shadow heard about this from the other trolls; word had spread fast around the castle. So when Bones was questioned, and Shadow found out it was true, he was furious. I heard he made him empty the pot to look for you."

"Okay, now we are all together we need to find out where Bones has taken everyone," Cherry said frantically.

Thorn said in a nervous little voice, "I know where Oakie and

Willow are. You see that mountain covered in heather? That's where they are."

"How do you know that?"

Thorn was just about to answer, when both Amy and Cherry said, "THE TROLLS!"

Thorn let out a tiny giggle and said, "Very good, oh you're good."

Cherry felt a leap in her heart. She knew they were only a spit away from the mountain and she could imagine them shouting for help, calling her name.

"Let's go!" Amy shouted, and she picked Thorn and Cherry up and carefully placed them in her pocket. As Amy crawled out of the hollow tree she noticed how dull everywhere was; the trees needed their fairies back. She could feel the trees' pain; their branches had no leaves and all the colour had been taken from them. It was horrible; she had never seen a tree look so bare and so sad. The whole forest was beginning to look bare, and so very glum. She knew she had to get those fairies back and stop Shadow once and for all.

Suddenly, there was a huge explosion at the top of the mountain. Thorn flew out of Amy's pocket in a panic, looking at the thick black smoke that filled the sky. Just the smell of it made him cough as it began to fill his tiny lungs. Amy grabbed him and put him back into her pocket. As Amy looked at the sky she began to feel fear welling up inside her, wondering if Oakie and Willow were okay or if they had been caught up in the explosion? She could feel her legs beginning to stiffen up.

As she walked up the long slope it felt like forever. Part of her wanted to give up and turn back, but she knew that Oakie and Willow depended on her; it was now or never. The life came back into her legs; she felt stronger than ever. As they got closer and closer to the mountain they could hear *BANG, BANG*. Suddenly another explosion occurred and Amy fell to the floor and covered her head. Thorn flew out of her pocket and told her to stay there. He flew to the edge of the cave and peered in. As he peered in it seemed to be too dark in there, but gradually his eyes became accustomed to it. It was then that he saw it. It was too horrible to describe; far too horrible even to mention! Perhaps he was mistaken; maybe it wasn't what he saw. It couldn't be, thought Thorn, not after such a long time. It couldn't be back, that's not possible. I saw him destroyed, thought Thorn. He took one more look; he jumped back and flew away from the cave as fast as he could, screaming at Amy, "RUN, RUN!"

Chapter Five

AMY RAN AS FAST AS she could. She turned around and saw that the mountain was far behind her. She had finally reached safety. Thorn flew past her and into the hollow tree. Amy reached the tree and crawled inside, puffing and panting with sheer exhaustion.

"What was that all about, Thorn? We are supposed to rescue them, not chicken out."

Thorn gasped. He tried to catch his breath, and frantically pointed to her pocket. Amy reached into her pocket and carefully took Cherry out, and sat her on a leafy bed. Cherry looked at Amy and then Thorn. She was very puzzled; one minute they were charging up to the mountain, the next minute charging back down. All she could say was, "Why are we back here?"

Thorn who had now caught up with his own breath, looked at Cherry and said, "I don't know how to tell you this … "

"Tell me what? WHAT, THORN? WHAT'S WRONG?" Cherry began to panic as Thorn hung his head and rubbed his eyes. He looked up and said, "Do you remember about a year ago Fairyland had this big monster named Death, and Queen Diamond fought him and banished him—he was destroyed, right?"

Cherry's face became rather serious. Her beautiful smile had gone; the sparkle in her eyes had also vanished.

"Yeah, Thorn, he was destroyed. I saw him and so did you. Why do you ask such a silly question?"

Thorn knew she was right as he had seen the battle and he knew Diamond had destroyed Death, but how could he be alive again? It didn't make any sense to Thorn. One thing was for certain, he was going to find out!

Cherry looked at Thorn and asked, "What's going on, Thorn?"

Thorn looked at Cherry and quickly said, "I think I've seen him, that's all."

Cherry was flabbergasted. She shook her head and shouted, "THAT'S ALL? THAT'S ALL?"

Amy butted in and said, "What's going on? Er, hello, would someone like to tell me what's going on? THORN! CHERRY! Somebody tell me."

Thorn looked at Amy and said in a very low voice, "I'll tell you."

Thorn began to clear his throat with a long cough. "Okay. It started about a year ago. Strange things were going on in Fairyland. Pixies were turning against us. They stopped being kind and wanting to help one another; they became self-centred. They started to turn ugly; their hearts became dark and black. Some wanted to become like Queen Diamond; they wanted her power just like Shadow did, and they wanted to become her. Slowly, more and more pixies joined them. They became so ugly they all grouped together and became one. Their power became great; six pixies became one person. Soon, all of Fairyland became afraid. Everyone was screaming as they could see different creatures coming for them. Amy, you have to understand this was very frightening for us; we did not know how to defeat it. His power was far greater than ours. There was only one person who knew how to defeat this creature and that was our beautiful Queen. You see, Fairyland is run by our Queen who gets her power from the Big Book."

"So how was this thing defeated then, Thorn?"

"Well, the Queen defeated him by the power of her word, the word from the Book. We try to live by this Book. That's why the

Book plays a big part in our lives. The secrets that lie within that Book are so powerful, they will blow your mind."

"I don't understand how he was defeated, then."

"Through the kindness that lies within the heart of the Book. As the Queen spoke the words from the Book, great big bolts of lightning pierced the heart of the creature. It screamed in agony; she spoke until finally it screamed its last breath. With a huge flash of light it was gone. And banished. Fairyland was restored back to its caring, loving self. That's how we have been living; it's been great up until now."

Cherry looked at Amy's face; she now had her mouth wide open in astonishment.

One thing Cherry and Thorn didn't understand was how Death could have come back. "What power had brought him back from nowhere?" they kept saying. "BUT HE WAS DESTROYED." One thing was for sure: it had to be stopped and destroyed again.

Amy looked at them and said, "Well, we can't rescue anyone while we are sitting in this tree; we must go and face this thing head on. No doubt we will find out how this thing reappeared, on our travels or from Oakie or Willow."

Amy put her hand out in front of her and Cherry and Thorn placed theirs on top of Amy's hand and shouted, "LET'S DO THIS!" They all laughed fearfully and crawled out of the hollow tree. Amy placed Cherry back into her pocket. Thorn insisted on flying next to her; he wanted to keep his wits about him. He needed to be up high to see in front of Amy, just in case anything was going to jump out on them or capture them. He was ready this time.

As they started to walk up the long pathway they could see the mountain getting closer and closer. Their hearts began to pound. Amy was very frightened. She didn't want to come face-to-face with this monster. She tried to calm herself down but it was no use. Her heart was beating louder than ever.

Finally they had arrived. The cave looked so dark; cobwebs

hung across the entrance. Amy noticed a big black spider that occupied the web. Yuck, thought Amy, as she felt a shiver run down her spine.

The darkness seemed to be beckoning them in. Amy felt drawn to walk inside as she took a step forward. Thorn put his hand on her shoulder and whispered, "Stay there; let me go first, like before." Thorn peered around the corner to see if the monster thing as they called it was still there. As his eyes got accustomed to the darkness he noticed that the monster had gone. Thorn had never been so relieved in all his life. He called to Amy, "All clear."

As Amy got close to the mouth of the cave she took a deep breath, wondering what lay ahead of her. She could feel her hands become more sweaty and slippery. She swallowed very hard as she stood by Thorn's side. Thorn turned to Amy and smiled a reassuring smile.

"It will be okay, Amy, you'll see," said Thorn.

She stared into the darkness, wondering if they would really be able to see. She took a deep breath and walked in.

Chapter Six

A s she walked in she heard a terrible scream, and fear struck her. Her footsteps became heavy; turning back was all she could think of. Suddenly the ground started to shake and Amy clung to the wall.

"What was that? I don't have a good feeling about this, Thorn."

As they went further into the cave, it seemed to split into three passages; one had a soft orange glow to it, which felt very warm and safe. Amy felt drawn to that one.

"I think we should go down this passage, Thorn, it looks so warm and cosy."

Amy felt a slight tug in her pocket, and she carefully took Cherry out, and sat her in her hand. They were all staring into the darkness of the other two passages. Cherry looked up at Amy with real fear in her eyes. The stench of the place smelt like death. Cherry began to tremble; she didn't like the look of the place, let alone the smell.

Cherry continued to stare down the other two passages, which were dark and damp. The sound of the dripping echoed loudly in Cherry's ears; all she could hear was *drip*, *drip* coming from the ceiling. Cherry placed her hands over her ears and began to tremble. Amy lovingly, and nervously, said, "It's going to be okay." She carefully placed Cherry back into her pocket. The orange glow seemed to be burning brighter as if telling them the way. Amy began walking towards the passage; a ghostly shadow ran across the walls. They both looked at each other but were unable to speak. Amy felt sheer terror run through her entire body.

Thorn blurted out, "THAT'S NOT THE RIGHT PASSAGE, IT'S A TRAP. RUN!"

Amy ran as fast as her legs would go; Thorn flew as fast as he could. They headed for the dark, damp, uninviting passage. Cherry peered out from Amy's pocket and quietly said, "I don't have a good feeling about this."

Suddenly it all became clear to Thorn that he had heard or read about orange glows, but where? He stopped and shouted out, "The Book!" Thorn thought to himself: If ever that book had gotten into the wrong hands, it would be disastrous!

Amy looked very puzzled. She turned to Thorn and said, "I heard everything you just said, or should I say *thought*."

Thorn now knew that she was the one; the one the Magical Book had been talking about, the one who would save Fairyland from Shadow and his evil realm. For the Book had said that "the one who is chosen, the one who is called, will be able to talk using their mind. For one so brave, the one so small will come and rescue your people. And she will bear a new name for she will be called The Warrior". Thorn had finally understood what that meant. The Book was talking about Amy.

Amy turned to Thorn and said, "We can talk with our minds now; it's much too dangerous not to. That way Shadow won't get to know any secrets about the Book."

Thorn and Cherry both agreed. Thorn pointed to the passage and using his mind said, "Let's carry on; I think we are nearly at the end."

As they got closer to the end of the passage they could see a tiny faint white light. They also could hear talking and screaming coming from somewhere. Cherry unfortunately knew the voice; the voice of Claw, one of Shadow's top right-hand men. She began to shake with fear; flashbacks of her being captured by

Bones and being tortured kept going through her mind. Amy had sensed something was wrong, and quietly whispered with a nervous voice, "I am here now."

Thorn told Amy to keep watch as he was going to fly ahead. As Thorn got closer to a dimly lit room he could see a cage, just like the one Cherry had been in, except this one was much smaller. He was sure he could see Willow but it was too dark to be certain. He could see a tiny shadow in the corner of the cage. He needed to get a closer look but had to wait for the right time. He could see that there was another passage that led somewhere. He would have to find out where it led to; perhaps Oakie was in there. He had to find out. He told Amy to keep watch; he loved using mind talk.

"Be careful," Amy had told him.

Thorn flew into the room. All he could hear was Claw laughing in his evil gruff voice. A chill ran down Thorn's back; he didn't like that sort of laugh. Thorn found a tiny hole in the wall, and he flew in and waited. Suddenly there was another loud thud, and in came Claw, laughing louder than ever which made the room shake. Thorn's mouth began to dry up; his palms felt sweaty. Fear had finally struck him. He noticed that Claw was holding something in his hand. When he looked closer, he noticed it was Oakie. All he wanted to do was shout to Oakie, but he knew he had to be quiet. He watched patiently.

"Hahahahahaha, you stupid pixie, I will pull your wings off if you don't tell me where that Book is."

"I will never tell you. I would rather go through my life never able to fly again. NEVER, I tell you, NEVER!"

"Very well, as you wish." Claw began to tie Oakie up. As he tied him up, Oakie could feel his tiny heart begin to pound. He began to wriggle to try and break free, but it was no use; the more he wriggled the tighter it became. Claw let out an evil laugh once more, and hung the rope onto the hook that was above his head. Thorn knew he had to tell Amy what he had just seen. But in his heart he wanted to rush in and try to rescue his wonderful friend. Flashbacks of Oakie haunted Thorn. He knew he had to do it now.

As he came out of his hiding place, he flew up to Oakie. Oakie began to shake his head.

"No, Thorn, get back, I'll be okay, get back. Quick, he's coming."

Thorn flew back into the hole just in time. And began to watch. It was too painful.

How could Oakie not want me to rescue him? thought Thorn. Screams rang through his ears; laughter echoed through the cave. As Thorn looked, he could see Claw pulling at Oakie's wings. It was horrible. All Thorn wanted to do was get far away from this beast. But he couldn't leave Oakie. Surely Claw had to stop. How far would this animal go? Thorn had to do something, but what? He began to talk to Amy using his mind; he began to call.

"Amy, Amy, can you hear me?"

"Yes, Thorn, I can hear you. What's wrong?"

Tears began to run down Thorn's cheeks as he began to tell Amy what was happening.

"Thorn," Amy said, "you have to get Oakie out as quickly as you can. Next time Claw leaves, you must grab him, or he'll, he'll ... well, you know."

"Yes, I know. I know what I have to do." Thorn could feel vengeance welling up inside him. He knew he had to control it or he too would be taken over by the darkness around him. Claw was shouting at Oakie, "Tell me where that Book is, or another wing goes." Oakie knew if he told him where the Book was, Fairyland had no hope. He had to protect his home, his friends, and the family he was yet to have. He bravely looked at Claw and shouted, "Pull it off, then, it's the last one anyway." Claw laughed. Thorn could tell that Claw loved every minute of it. He grabbed Oakie's wing and began to tug. As he tugged, Thorn remembered he still had some invisible potion to drink. As he drank he began to disappear. Finally he flew out of the hole as quick as lightning. He found a huge metal spike, and without a second thought began to say, "Metal rods become like lead, fall on his head and make him dead."

The rod rose up from the floor and fell down onto Claw's big ugly green scaly head. He fell to the floor, leaving Oakie weak and trembling with fear. Thorn reappeared and untied Oakie. Tears of joy and tears of pain ran down Oakie's cheeks."We must take you back to Amy," Thorn said.

All Oakie could do was smile and say, "We must find Willow; he is somewhere in here. We can't leave him."

"Don't worry, we will get him soon."

As they returned to Amy's side Oakie felt safe and he knew everything would be all right. Amy looked at the injured pixie and carefully placed him in her other pocket.

"We have to get him back to Fairyland somehow."

Chapter Seven

SUDDENLY THERE WAS A LOUD roar, and the ground began to shake. Amy shouted at Thorn, "I thought Claw was dead! Thorn, what happened? He's still alive!"

Thorn began to panic as the loud roar was getting closer. All Amy could say was, "RUN! RUN!" She began to run, and Thorn flew as fast as his wings could go. Fear was driving them. They came to a dead end. There was nowhere to run, nowhere to hide. They were stuck. Amy lifted Cherry out of her pocket and sat her on her shoulder.

The roars seemed to be getting closer; soon they would be face to face with this hideous monster. Cherry quickly asked Thorn, "Did you have vengeance in your heart when you made the spell?" Thorn looked at Cherry and began to remember how he hated Claw.

"YES, YES, I did, I hated him for what he did to Oakie. Why was that a problem? I needed to rescue him. That monster pulled his wings off. You should have seen it. It was horrible."

"Yes, I know he did, but didn't you learn anything from the Book? Only a person with a pure heart can defeat evil. And it can't be us; we're too involved. We're going to be protective, of course. It's only natural. That's why it has to be Amy: *Only the heart of a child.*"

It all became very clear to Thorn. How could I have been so stupid? he thought. I should have known. I have put us all in great danger.

Amy began to panic. The roars were getting closer; too close for Amy's liking.

"What am I supposed to do? I can't do spells," she shouted.

Claw was now in sight. Amy began to scream, he was so ugly. Thorn now began to shout, "NOW, AMY, NOW, BEFORE IT'S TOO LATE. NOW, I TELL YOU, NOW!"

Claw seemed to have reached them very quickly. "Hahahahahaha," he roared. "Now I have you trapped. There's nowhere to hide; you're mine now."

Claw gave one big swoop and knocked Amy across the room. Amy could hardly move; fear had taken her over; her legs felt like jelly. As she looked up she could see Cherry on the floor, begging for her life. Thorn had been captured and was clenched in Claw's claw. Amy knew she had to act fast before Claw ate her friend, who was already being held up in the air and dangling in Claw's mouth.

Thorn screamed loudly as he could see the inside of Claw's mouth; his green slimy teeth and smelly breath were enough. Thorn began to wriggle and shout, "HURRY UP, AMY. NOW! I CAN'T STAND THE SMELL. NOW!!"

All of a sudden, as if by magic, her mouth opened and she began to shout, "Rocks fall from the sky, and fall on Claw's head, and make him DEAD!"

There was a loud rumble, and rocks began to hit him. He fell to the floor, releasing Thorn from his mighty grip. Thorn flew free as fast as he could.

As Claw lay there he began to disintegrate. Amy didn't know what to say. One thing was for sure: she was very pleased with herself. Cherry began to cheer. Oakie was still too weak to know what was going on, but you could tell by his face that he was pleased. Another thing was for sure: he had to get home.

Amy looked at Thorn and said, "Why doesn't Cherry take Oakie back to Fairyland? She can use a spell to transport them both back to Thorn's house. We can carry on the journey."

Cherry looked at Thorn and smiled. Amy took Oakie out of her pocket and gave him to Cherry. As Cherry took Oakie in her arms she quietly whispered, "Be brave, we will soon be home." Thorn smiled a half smile as Cherry began to chant, "Somewhere to hide, somewhere safe, take me back to Thorn's place." As quick as a flash Cherry and Oakie were back at Thorn's mushroom. Cherry walked over and placed Oakie onto the bed. As she walked away from the bed something caught her eye out of the window; she noticed that Oakie's tree had a tiny patch of colour. She wondered if her tree had colour too. It won't be long now before all your colour has fully returned, she thought to herself. I have him here.

Amy began to feel uneasy as if someone was watching them. She turned to Thorn and said, "Which way?"

"We need to go into the room that held Oakie," said Thorn.

"Didn't you see another room in there?"

"We need to see if Willow is anywhere in there," said Thorn.

Thorn suddenly remembered the cage that had hung above Claw's head; he remembered seeing a tiny shadow in the corner of the cage. Could that have been Willow? Surely not. How could Willow have not shouted for me? he thought. Thorn was very puzzled. As he looked around for the way back he could see a tunnel. He knew the way.

"This way, Amy," shouted a very excited Thorn.

They both set off to finish the rest of the quest. They were nearly at the end of the tunnel when Amy said, "Do you feel like someone is watching us?"

"No," replied Thorn.

Amy didn't like this feeling; she had never had it before. They finally reached the room that had held Oakie. Thorn instantly looked up. He could see the cage. He flew up to it and saw a tiny mouse shivering with fear.

"Who are you?" shouted Thorn.

"My … my … my name's Brownie."

Brownie

"Have you seen my friend Willow, Brownie? And why are you trapped inside this cage?" asked Thorn with an inquisitive manner.

Amy decided to investigate the other room. As she walked in, she could see drawings of lots of cages and lots of mice too. As she studied the papers she could see words mixed in between the mice. How very strange, she thought. She noticed there seemed to be a funny smell, like burning. Amy looked around but could see nothing burning. How odd, she thought. Just then, Amy noticed some scratches written on the wall. She moved closer to take a good look; she noticed it was a message. The message read,

Being taken to a lighted cave. Beware.
W.

Hmm, thought Amy. 'W' could stand for Willow. She became rather excited.

Amy came running out of the room shouting about the papers she had found and, more importantly, shouting, "I KNOW WHERE WILLOW HAS BEEN TAKEN!"

"Is Willow a pixie, like you?" asked Brownie.

"Yes," replied Thorn.

Thorn flew down to Amy and questioned her. She told him all about the scratched message that was written on the wall.

"Are you sure it was from Willow?"

"Only one way to find out," replied Amy.

Thorn flew back up and opened the cage door. "Come on, Brownie, you're coming with us."

"Yippee. Oh thank you, thank you!" screamed Brownie in his mouse-like voice.

Amy had just one question for their new little friend.

"Brownie, I noticed drawings on the wall with cages and lots of mice. What were they for?"

Brownie shuddered. "I really don't feel comfortable talking about this, but since you've asked I will tell you. There's a huge monster that is somewhere in this cave. He is left to roam around; his name is Death. Well, you see, us mice are his ... his ... his food. Okay, now you know! The trolls would leave us mice in the cages so when the monster roamed in the different rooms he would take the mouse and gobble him up."

Amy's mouth dropped open as she realised that the monster could be anywhere.

"Okay," replied Thorn. "I know all about this monster and he's not to be messed with. Let's go to the cave of light."

Brownie's face changed. Amy and Thorn could see pure fear and dread in his eyes He began to tremble.

"What's up, little guy?" Amy bent down and picked him up to comfort him.

"That's where the monster was not that long ago."

She really didn't want to meet this monster. But they were Willow's only hope. She had to be brave.

Chapter Eight

As they came to the lighted cave, Amy's heart began to race. They were just about to walk in when Brownie stopped them.

"Don't go in there. I know a better way." He looked at Amy and said, "One problem. You will never fit on my back. You need to shrink, and then you will be able to get on."

Amy remembered the shrinking potion. She reached into her backpack and brought out a tiny bottle. She began to drink, and as she drank so she shrank. They both climbed onto Brownie's back and he ran through a tiny little hole in the wall, only big enough for a fat mouse. As they went in, Amy was suddenly aware that everything looked huge. The room was well lit with diagrams all over the walls.

Hmm, thought Amy. She wanted to take a closer look, but Brownie still carried on walking.

"Nearly there," he said.

Amy still felt like she was being watched, and she felt even worse now she was tiny. Monster food was all she could think of. What she didn't know was that she *was* being watched. Shadow was looking at her through his cauldron. Shadow had become very angry as the news had travelled fast about Claw's death. One of Shadow's top right-hand men had been defeated. He was very angry and wanting vengeance.

"You're walking straight into my trap. Ahhhhh! BOYS, BOYS!" shouted Shadow.

Bones and Snake came pounding in.

"YES, BOSS?" They both stood waiting for Shadow to give his next command.

"Go and give our little friends a wonderful surprise. Bring out DEATH!! FOR NO ONE, I TELL YOU, NO ONE WILL EVER DEFEAT ME. I AM UNSTOPPABLE. FAIRYLAND WILL BE MINE." Shadow let out a really evil laugh, so evil that it sent a chill down Bones' spine.

"Yes, boss," they both said.

Bones and Snake ran down the corridor, laughing and chanting, "Death, Death, we have some food for you, nice little fairy food, ahahhahhhhahh. Come with us and we will take you to them."

Suddenly the ground began to shake. Snake finally caught sight of him. He had never seen anything so evil; his big red glowing eyes seemed to burn right into Snake's very soul. His tall black figure smelt of sulphur. As he walked he left a black trail of thick smoke like smog behind him. Snake was filled with fear as this was the first time he had ever seen him.

Bones laughed and said, "Death, you have to go and find Amy and that stupid fairy, Thorn. Shadow wants them gone. I think you know what I mean by *gone*, don't you, boy?"

Death gave the deepest and most evil laugh. It seemed to make the whole cave shake. As he walked past Snake, Death looked at him and stared right into his soul and laughed.

"I hate him. He gives me the creeps," Snake said.

"Wait till you see what he will do to the others. He will destroy them, he will take their souls, and they will be no more."

As Brownie was walking, Amy noticed how soft he was as she stroked his fur. He was brown with white patches on his sides; he had the sweetest little pink nose she had ever seen. She loved how he twitched his whiskers as he walked, his little pink paws scurrying across the ground. She could understand why he was called Brownie. Even still, she would have called him Soft Brownie.

They finally stopped at the entrance to the glowing cave. Amy was captivated by the strange light that seemed to come from nowhere. Diagrams and strange drawings were all over the walls just like all the other rooms, but what did they all mean?

Amy looked at all the drawings and stumbled upon something really fascinating.

"Thorn, come here, I've found something."

Thorn flew over to see what she had found. In his heart he had hoped it would be Willow. As he looked at the drawing he noticed it wasn't just a drawing; it was a spell that linked up to make a picture.

"We must find all the pictures, then we will know what the spell makes," Thorn said.

They collected all the drawings from around the walls. They sat on the floor and started to put the picture together. Thorn shouted, "We need three more pieces. It's useless without them!"

Amy remembered the other room had pictures around the walls too. "We need to go back to the other room where we found Oakie."

"It's no good. There's no time if we go back," Thorn said.

Brownie bravely said, "I'll go. You carry on looking for Willow and I will go back to get the other drawings." Amy and Thorn agreed. Brownie turned tail and ran through the hole in the wall.

As Thorn studied the pictures he had a horrible feeling come over him. In his heart he knew what the pictures were and what they meant. In a way he didn't want Brownie to come back with the rest of the pictures. He didn't want his fears confirmed.

As Brownie came running back through the hole, in his mouth were the pictures that they were looking for.

"I mav em," Brownie said.

"Mav em? What does that mean?" Amy laughed.

Brownie gave the pictures to Thorn and looked at Amy and sarcastically said, "Mav em, smarty pants, means 'have them'.

I am sorry, I can't speak proper English when I have something in my mouth."

Thorn started placing the missing pictures together, and realised that his worst nightmares had been confirmed. Shadow had recreated Death. Thorn quietly said to himself, "Amy, I know what Shadow has done."

"What? What has he done? Please tell me."

"Do you remember I told you about how our Queen had defeated the monster, how he was banished and died? Everyone in Fairyland saw him die. Well, Shadow has used the recreating spell. This picture shows Death. It also shows us the spell. As the spell is spoken out so the monster comes back to life and back from banishment. We are in great danger."

Amy was shocked by this. Suddenly, the ground began to shake and the picture started to move. BOOM. BOOM. There it was again. It seemed to be getting closer and closer.

Chapter Nine

"**W**HAT IS IT, THORN?"

Thorn looked around for somewhere to hide or to see if he could see Willow anywhere.

"JUMP ON, YOU TWO, JUMP ON!" Brownie shouted.

Amy and Thorn jumped on his back. Brownie turned tail and ran as fast as he could, but just as Brownie could see the hole in the wall, just when they could almost smell safety, that's when they saw it. It was so frightening to even look at. Amy let out a huge scream, and Thorn covered her mouth quickly.

"Don't look into his eyes. If you do he will keep your soul and destroy it. Run, Brownie, run," shouted Thorn.

The big black figure towered above them; he seemed to follow them no matter where they ran. They could not get away. Amy was trying not to look at him, which was really hard as his big red eyes seemed to be drawing hers to his.

"Close your eyes, Amy. Close them now or you'll be gone forever!" screamed Thorn.

Amy closed her eyes tight, not wanting to look at the black ghastly figure, as Death's big black hand reached down to swoop and crush them.

Brownie found another hole; this time it was not in the wall but the floor. Brownie shouted, "Hold on as tight as you can. I don't know where this will lead." His little legs were running as fast as he could; he ran right through Death's legs and jumped into the hole. Both Amy and Thorn held on to Brownie for dear life. The hole seemed to go down into a spiral. Round and round they went, down and down. Amy and Thorn held on, pulling on poor Brownie's fur.

"Ouch, you guys, don't pull so hard."

Finally they had come to a standstill. "Can I open my eyes now?" Amy asked.

"Yes, Amy, we are safe now; well, at least I think we are anyway. We seem to be in an underground cave. Not sure where we are really."

Thorn looked around and scratched his head. I wonder where we are, he thought. I've never seen this place before. Amy got off Brownie and gazed in amazement. Around the walls were tiny gems, and the floor seemed to be made of pure gold. There was one chair in the middle of the room; a long red carpet flowed from the chair's base as if waiting for someone important. Amy looked carefully at the chair; she noticed a lion's head carved on the arm of the chair, and rubies were encrusted in its head. Around the walls were paintings of kings and queens, princes and princesses; their wings looked like they were made from pure silk, as if, by magic, a spider had been at work. It was amazing. Amy had never seen such a beautiful picture. For the first time she felt safe, kind of like a safe house she never wanted to leave.

"Where are we, Thorn, do you know? What is this place? It's simply beautiful!" Amy said.

"No. I have never seen this place before. It would seem that we are safe indeed. One thing I would like to know: can Death reach us in here? Or is this a trap to lead us somewhere where we feel safe, then capture us and torture us? I feel this is a set-up. I wish Cherry was here. She would know; she knows everything."

Amy smiled a big and wide smile; she had a brilliant idea."Why don't we use our minds to talk to her? This way we can see how Oakie is doing, and find out what this place is."

Thorn started to think and talk in his mind.

"Cherry, can you hear me? Cherry, can you hear me? It's

Thorn; we need your help."

"I can hear you. What's wrong? I thought you would never get in touch. I was so worried about you."

"Sorry. I have found out some really important stuff."

"Like what, Thorn?"

"Well, I know Shadow has recreated Death and brought him back from banishment. We have just escaped in time. Brownie got us out and he slid down this hole in the floor. It's amazing, Cherry, this room is made from pure gold and there's a single chair in the room with a red carpet. Do you know where we are? And if we are safe?"

There was silence for a moment. Thorn began to worry and think this was not a safe place. He was just about to suggest they get out of there when Cherry shouted, with great joy, "Thorn, you know where you are, don't you? Oh, I wish I could see this. I've only heard about it in the Big Book. How wonderful for you."

"Forget about how wonderful it is. We need to know. Where we are?"

Cherry snapped, "Thorn, don't be so impatient. The room you are in belonged to the Fairy kings and queens of long ago. On the walls are pictures of who they where, and what they did for Fairyland. Some died defending the Book. Only on a certain day and at a certain time will the Chief Fairy King appear. It is the greatest privilege in all of Fairyland to see him on that day. You must have had a personal invite."

"How come? I don't understand. We've not seen him."

"No, but he obviously made the hole appear, silly. You see, not one person has even found the room. It was as if it never existed. Many fairies and pixies through our time had even doubted it was all true."

"Thanks, Cherry. Now I know at least we are safe. How is Oakie? Is he any better?"

"He's fine, getting stronger. One thing I will say: be careful. Don't stay in there too long, otherwise Death may find you, then he will destroy—or at least try to destroy—the room. He wants to pay Diamond back for defeating him and banishing him many moons ago. Stay strong and stay focused on the mission in hand. You can do this, you all can."

Suddenly, there was a bright light that surrounded the whole room. Amy and Thorn covered their eyes as the light was so bright. Standing in front of the chair was a man. His clothes were beautifully made from silk and gold. On his head he wore a golden crown with many beautiful gemstones encrusted into it. The crown was truly an amazing sight. Amy, Brownie, and Thorn instantly fell to the floor.

"You may arise."

As they stood up, his face was so beautiful. Down one side it glittered. Fairy dust, thought Thorn. This must be the Fairy King.

"That is correct, young Thorn, I am Gemstone the Mighty. It is my understanding that Death has been released. You do understand that he will be more powerful than ever before. This is why I am giving you this mighty sword. It is by the power of this sword you will be able to defeat him."

As he handed Thorn the magnificent sword, the power that was within it ran straight through Thorn's body. Thorn had never experienced anything like it.

"Thank you, Your Majesty, I will take care of this sword."

"I know you will. And to young brave little Amy; I will give you the gift of wisdom, for you will know when to attack and when to stay back. Take this shield. It will protect you on your way. Young Brownie, my little fat mouse, I will equip you with body armour. I give you the helmet to protect your face, the armour to protect your body, and these little shoes to protect your feet. I give you the gift of strength to be able to carry the two warriors to complete their journey. I will also give you an army. But only I will know when you truly need it. We shall have many meetings and I will summon you back to this room. I know Cherry had told you that Death could find you, but I tell you this room cannot be found unless I reveal it. Only until then."

The King pointed his hand towards the gold walls, and from his fingertips shone a light so bright, the wall completely disappeared.

"Go and complete your journey. You will face many dangers, trials and tribulations, but you will complete it and become victorious. Now, go and save Fairyland."

As the three of them walked into the bright light, so the King disappeared. They all stared at each other, wondering if it had really happened or whether they'd just imagined it all. Everything seemed far too real. As they looked down they could see the great gifts the King had bestowed upon them. They realised it had really happened. Fear no longer reigned in them, but strength and character, and most of all, boldness.

Chapter Ten

THEY FOUND THEMSELVES IN A room, a room too dark to see anything. Amy, wanting to make sure they were all still together, began to shout, "Thorn, Brownie, are you there?"

"Yes," they replied.

Thorn remembered the torch he had in his knapsack. He reached inside and took it out. He flicked the switch and shone it around the room. He caught sight of Amy and Brownie. They began to look around the room and they could hear a faint voice crying out, saying, "HELP ME. I can see your light. Please, you must help me." Thorn knew that voice, but where was it coming from?

"We need more light; we need more light," Thorn said in a panic.

"Okay, I heard you the first time. I'll get my torch out," replied a rather frustrated Amy. She reached into her backpack and found her torch, flicked the switch ... and bingo, the room was filled with light. Amy could now see something rather strange. She found four mirrors all in a circle. Hmm, she thought, forgetting Thorn was tuned into her thoughts, I wonder what these are for? He said, "Looks rather strange, doesn't it, but helpful. Shine your torch onto one just to see what will happen. Looks like something I've seen before but can't quite think where or how."

Amy shone her torch onto the first mirror, and as she did, the light reflected onto one of the other mirrors, then another, and another, lighting up all four. The room filled with light. Instead of being in what they thought was a small room, it was now a huge room filled with statues of trolls and evil goblins.

"Yuck! These are horrid," said Amy. As she looked closer at one of the mirrors she could see a reflection of someone very frightened.

"THORN! You have to look at this. I've found something, or should I say someone."

Thorn came over to investigate, hoping it was Willow, and as he looked into the mirror he shouted, "It's Marigold! Amy, you found Marigold!" Thorn flew up to Amy and kissed her on her forehead.

"Someone special was she, then?"

"No," replied Thorn.

"Mmm," laughed Amy. As she looked closer she saw something which caught her eye. She could see that Marigold was trapped inside the mirror, but the mirror was in a different room.

"Mmm, how interesting, a mirror within a mirror," she said to herself.

"So how do we get her out, smarty pants?"

"Of that, my dear Thorn, I have no idea. I was hoping you would know."

Amy suddenly heard a voice cry out, 'Smash the mirror."

"Yes, I know that, Brownie, but it would make a noise and alert the trolls."

"Not if you place your coat over the mirror. It'll muffle the sound. Try it."

Amy looked at Brownie and said, "Okay, if you say so. I just hope it works." She immediately took off her coat, laid it over the mirror and quietly said to Thorn, "Smash the mirror with your sword. Come on, smash it." Thorn raised the sword in the air and swung it hard into the mirror. They all looked at each other as, to their surprise, the mirror hadn't smashed. Amy carefully took her coat off and noticed there was a big crack in the middle of the mirror.

"Why has it only cracked, Amy?" asked a very puzzled mouse.

"Don't know, Brownie."

Thorn looked into the mirror and saw Marigold was trying to say something. "Sshh, everyone, stop talking, she's trying to tell us something."

As Amy and Brownie stopped talking, so Marigold shouted, "SHINE YOUR TORCH ONTO THE MIRROR."

"We've done that already," said Amy.

"Do it again and you will see what will happen, but you must lay your coat back over the mirror. You must trust me." Those words began ringing in Amy's ears. "Trust me" was all she could hear.

"Okay , let's try it." Amy laid her coat back over the mirror and shone her torch onto her coat; suddenly there was a loud SMASH. Glass was everywhere.

"Be careful, Brownie. Don't cut your little pink feet."

"I have my special shoes on, Amy, but thank you."

Amy was waiting for some trolls to appear, but when they never came, she carefully took her coat off the mirror. To their amazement, within the mirror frame was in fact another room. Amy stepped into the mirror frame and looked around. She had soon realised she was alone, and she looked back at Thorn and Brownie and said, "Are you two coming?"

As Thorn and Brownie stepped through the frame they looked around at a very strange cavern. Thorn frantically said, "Where's Marigold?"

"Mmm, that's what I would like to know. I thought once the mirror was smashed she would fall out of the thing."

Brownie began to point his nose in the air and sniffed. He could smell something that smelt like flowers.

"What's up, boy, what can you smell?" asked Amy.

"Flowers, Amy, that's what I can smell, and it seems to be coming from over here."

Thorn got very excited and shouted, "That's Marigold; she lives in the flowers and always smells like them. Where is she, boy? Take us to her."

Brownie led them to yet another mirror. "Oh no, not another one!" shouted Thorn, very angrily.

"Calm down, Thorn. You are no good to anyone angry, are you now?"

Thorn looked through the mirror and saw his wonderful friend. "Get ready to catch her, Amy." Amy stood close to the mirror, waiting for Thorn to smash it.

"Stand back." He raised his sword and smashed the mirror, and it shattered into a thousand pieces. Marigold fell out and landed, thankfully, in Amy's hands.

"Thank you," she said in a quiet voice.

Chapter Eleven

AMY COULD HEAR THE MOST piercing sound; she knew instantly what it was. She knew that Thorn had triggered the alarm off.

"Thorn, you didn't place my coat over the mirror, did you?"

"Oh no, I forgot! I was so concerned in getting Marigold out that I forgot to."

"Well done. We have now alerted the trolls. That sound is an alarm. We have to get out of here, but how or where?

"Thorn, we have to leave before we get a dozen trolls in here."

Suddenly the ground began to shake and they could hear footsteps getting closer and closer. They could hear the trolls grunting and snarling, the sound of their weapons clanging together as they ran. Amy looked for another way out but there was nowhere to go. Amy looked at Thorn, held her shield in the air, and said, "Together we fight."

Thorn felt the special moment, and held his sword in the air and said, "Together we stand." Brownie knew he just had to join in and said, "Together we are strong." They felt the power run through their bodies as they stood there and waited for the trolls to come. Thorn drew his sword and stood in a fighting stance. Brownie got ready for them to jump on his back if they needed a quick getaway, and Amy held her shield up ready for battle.

The grunting sounds were now on top of them. In came the trolls, laughing. They were ghastly. Some were green and some were blackish-brown, with big tufts of hair coming from their ears. The stench was enough to knock anyone out. They smelt a bit like rotten cabbage mixed in with a hint of wet dog. They had green slime coming out of their noses, and on the end of each of their noses was a great big wart. The trolls laughed as they stood there. Bones stepped out and said in an evil, gruff voice, "Well, well, boys, what do we have here? Four wannabe heroes, ahhhhhh, and look what they have caught for us. Another stupid fairy."

"Yeah, Bones, the boss is going to be so proud of us for bringing these back to him."

"Yeah, yeah, yeah," said one of the trolls. Thorn raised his sword bravely. Bones laughed at the sight.

"Oh look, Snake, the little fairy wants a fight." All the trolls laughed and sneered at them. Thorn raised his sword higher in the air; this made the trolls laugh even harder.

"What's the fairy going to do with that tiny sword, boys? I think he's trying to harm us big powerful trolls, ahhhhhhh. We could knock him over with just one big sneeze."

As Bones stood there, Amy noticed that the green slime that was hanging from the end of his nose was getting bigger and slimier. He glared at them while wiping it off with his big green scaly hand. Now he had it hanging from the ends of his fingers. He looked at it hanging off, laughed, and put his fingers into his mouth.

"That's disgusting!" Amy shouted.

Thorn looked at Bones and said, "This sword may look tiny but it's very powerful and can take you trolls right out of the game."

"Aw, Furball, did you hear that! I've never heard anything so stupid in all my life."

Why they call him Furball I will never know, thought Amy.

"Use your sword, Thorn, use it now!" shouted Amy and Marigold. "Don't listen to the trolls; they are only trying to put you off."

Thorn's arm began to fall back to his side. As it did, he remembered what the King had given Amy; and her gift was wisdom. He knew he had to listen to her. He stretched out his arm again, this time straight up in the air. The top of the sword suddenly glowed bright red. The trolls were startled and began to back off a little.

"Aw, what's wrong, boys, getting worried?" laughed Brownie.

The trolls screamed at them and ran forward, charging at them with clubs and heavy chains swinging in the air. Bolts of lightning shot from the tip of the sword. The trolls flew across the room and landed in a heap in the corner. As Thorn lowered his sword his three friends and himself were teleported to a different room. They all looked at each other in amazement.

"What just happened back there, Amy?" Thorn asked in a very puzzled manner.

"You showed the trolls, that's what happened."

Brownie shouted, jumping up and down in excitement. "Stupid trolls, stupid trolls!"

"Brownie, that's quite enough," laughed Amy.

"Thorn, did you know that the sword would glow red and shoot out bolts of lightning? Did you know the sword could teleport us?"

"No, Amy, I didn't. I have a feeling that this sword will do lots of different things. But did you see the trolls go flying across the room? Awesome!"

As they came back to reality and the excitement wore off, they realised they were in yet another room. Amy liked this room as there were plenty of holes in the walls and in the floors; plenty of places to run if need be. Marigold, in her sweet little voice, quietly said, "Thorn, we still have to find Willow. How can we find him in here?"

"Hmm," said Thorn.

Suddenly the sword started to glow yellow. As it glowed, so pictures started to appear in the sword. Amy and Thorn turned to each other in amazement. They looked into the blade and saw a circle with a ring of fire around it and in the middle of the ring was Willow, looking scared and worried. One question they all had was, where was this Ring of Fire?

Chapter Twelve

THE SWORD STARTED TO SHOW yet another picture, but this time it showed a cave with moss around the outside. The cave looked similar to the one where they'd found Oakie. "I knew it. I knew he was back at that cave where Oakie was. I could sense it. It's called fairy power."

"Thorn, you are funny. There's no such thing as fairy power, you silly thing," laughed Marigold.

As they looked at the sword they noticed it had stopped glowing, and as Thorn bent down to pick it up, reaching out to grab it, he noticed that the sword was generating heat. A heat he couldn't touch. Looking down to his feet he could see the rock floor was melting and falling away below them. Each of them tried to find part of the wall to frantically hold on to. Thinking it was the end for them, they fell down into a big dark hole. Their screams echoed around the black pit.

"Where are we?" they all said together.

As Amy brushed herself down she frantically asked, "Is everyone okay?" Out from the darkness tiny voices began to say, "Yeah, we're okay." They stood in silence for a while before Amy said, "We need light." As she said "we need light", so the sword shone a brilliant white beam which gave them light.

"Wow," they all said in such wonder.

The pit turned out to be not a pit but a tunnel. There was nothing in the tunnel except more passages. Thorn reached out again to pick up his sword, hesitating to see if it was still hot. As he stretched out his hand he could feel that it had cooled down very quickly.

"Amy, I think this sword is very special."

"YOU THINK? Thorn, I had no idea!" Amy said very sarcastically.

"Enough of that! We need to find our way out of here," said Brownie. "Jump on my back."

As they all climbed on Brownie's back he felt a surge of power run through his tiny body. He felt as strong as an ox; he felt good. He began to run down the long tunnel, and as he ran, he felt heat being generated from somewhere. Sweat began to run down Brownie's face. Hmm, he thought.

"Guys, can you feel that heat or am I just getting a hot flush?" he said. "I don't think mice get hot flushes, but I am."

As Brownie stopped, Amy got off and stood by him; she carefully stretched out her hand and felt a great heat.

"I think we've found it, the Ring of Fire."

They were all very excited. Brownie noticed a very familiar smell.

"Er, guys, don't get too excited. My supersonic mouse nose has picked up a smell that's a bit like TROLLS."

Thorn lifted his sword in the air and said, "Show us the entrance to the Ring of Fire." The sword flew out of Thorn's hand and began to hover in the air and glow yellow again. Pictures began forming on the blade, revealing that the entrance to the Ring of Fire was guarded by two horrid-looking trolls.

"Haven't seen these ones before," said Amy. "You're the top mouse; your nose is really something."

Thorn held his hand up in the air and the sword floated down into it. Once again the sword and Thorn were one. They all slowly moved forward down the tunnel. The heat was becoming unbearable.

"How Willow has survived this heat I will never know," said a rather worried Marigold.

Suddenly they came face to face with two ugly trolls with big clubs in their hands. Their faces were big and fat and green, and their ears were big and pointed at the ends, with big tufts of fur coming out of them. Their eyes were orange and black. One had a nose a bit like a dog, long and pointed; the other had a tiny but strange sort of squashed nose. They both had huge warts on the tip of them. Their feet were big and dumpy with claws that looked razor-sharp; their hands were the same.

"Look, Wolf, look what we have here," said Thud, the first one.

"Yeah, look," snorted Wolf.

They lifted their clubs up and swung at them, but missed. Amy couldn't help but giggle; these must be the stupidest trolls she had ever seen.

"Hahaha, you missed them, Wolf."

"Will you stop snorting, Thud? I know I missed them."

Amy couldn't believe her ears; now they were arguing about who missed who. As the trolls carried on arguing, Thud swung his club into Wolf's head. He went plummeting to the ground. Wolf got up and pushed Thud half way across the room, sending him into the next cavern. Thorn had his fill of them arguing.

"THAT'S ENOUGH, I'VE HAD ENOUGH!" screamed Thorn. He lifted his sword and thrust it deep into Wolf's gut. As he pulled the sword out so green slime came out too. As they watched, they had never seen anything like it; the sword had caused him to become disfigured. He began to swell up and up, just like a balloon. The other troll, who had been watching from a distance, ran for his life. He didn't want what was happening to his friend to happen to him. As they carried on looking they noticed his face was sliding down towards his tummy; the troll was screaming in agony.

Suddenly Thorn shouted, "RUN, RUN! He's GOING TO BLOW!" They all began to run but it was no use. The troll blew up, leaving Thorn and Amy, Marigold and Brownie covered in green slime.

"Oh YUCK! That's disgusting," they all said, flicking the slime off themselves.

Amy had slime in her hair and it was running down her back.

"You could have warned us, Thorn, that it would do that!" shouted Amy and Brownie.

Brownie carried on flicking the slime off his tail and feet. Marigold laughed as she looked at everyone all slimy and green.

"I am pleased you can see the funny side. Just look at us, we're green," Amy moaned. Thorn said nothing. He thought it was best not to as Amy was so angry. As Thorn took off his hat, he tipped it upside down and slime poured out of it. Marigold had slime all down her back but she didn't seem bothered like Amy.

"Come on, guys, we have to find Willow," Thorn begged. They all began to walk further into the heat towards the Ring of Fire, and as they stared through the flames, they found Willow lying on the floor within the circle, as if dead.

"We're too late! We're too late!" Marigold said in a croaky voice.

Amy wondered how they would put the fire out. There was no water anywhere. Thorn hoped the sword could somehow do it. Thorn looked at his sword, which was also dripping with the slime, and shouted.

"Sword, put the fire out!" The sword started to glow blue and the room became cold. They all became *very* cold; their teeth started to chatter; they all cuddled themselves and rubbed their hands together.

"Thorn, why is it so cold in here? It's freezing," Brownie chattered.

Thorn was unable to hold the sword and dropped it. As it began to fall, so what looked like millions of tiny icicles came away from it and landed on the fire. Instantly the fire went out. Everyone was amazed. The icicles had melted away and the room started to warm up.

"Thank goodness. I was beginning to get icicles on my tail," laughed a very relieved Brownie.

Marigold walked into the circle and picked Willow up. A single tear ran down her cheek and landed onto Willow's forehead, but still nothing happened.

"We've lost him. We were too late," sobbed Marigold.

The sword began to glow a bright purple and they all disappeared. When they arrived they noticed that they were back in the Throne Room, with the King standing in front of his throne just like before. Placing Willow gently and lovingly onto the ground, they all fell to the floor in respect.

"You may arise. I see you have found the power that lies within the sword."

"Yes, Your Majesty, but we lost one of the pixies," sobbed Thorn.

"Aww, young Willow. Am I correct?"

"Yes, you're correct."

"Please carry him to me."

Marigold picked up Willow's lifeless little body from the ground and passed him to Gemstone. As she placed Willow into the King's hand, he lifted Willow up to his face and blew on him. As he blew, so fairy dust came from his mouth and covered Willow's face. Suddenly Willow opened his eyes and sat up and said, "Where am I? I'm hungry." Everyone rejoiced. The King pointed his finger to an open space by the wall and a beam of light shone from his finger just like before. But instead of the wall disappearing, food appeared. They could not believe their eyes; Thorn had to rub his to make sure he wasn't dreaming. This was a banquet with all types of food. There was roast chicken for Amy, and for the fairies much smaller food, like berries and wild honey. Willow tucked in as did they all. It tasted wonderful; just what they all needed.

The King looked at them, smiled and said, "My friends, I think it would be safer for Willow and Marigold to stay with me, as they will rejoin you for the final battle. Eat plenty and enjoy while you can. You have many more adventures ahead of you. The sword will do many more amazing things, and will help you on your journey."

Chapter Thirteen

T HEY HAD JUST FINISHED EATING when the King pointed his finger at Thorn and Amy, and a brilliant white light came from his fingertips just like before. But instead of the wall disappearing, Amy and Thorn did.

"Where are we now?" Amy said.

Looking around, she noticed that she seemed to be in a sleeping volcano, and all alone, as Thorn was nowhere to be seen. Amy began to panic. She shouted, "THORN! THORN! WHERE ARE YOU?" But only silence greeted her call. Now Amy was panicking and she started imagining all sorts of bad things. Her mind had been completely taken over by her fear, and she began frantically searching behind the big lava rocks, but found nothing. She let out another loud cry.

"THORN, OH, THORN, please talk to me."

All of a sudden she heard a faint voice say, "I am down here."

"Down where? I can't see you anywhere."

"Over here. Over here. Look down, look down, I tell you."

As Amy followed Thorn's voice she noticed a small crater ahead. She gingerly looked down inside and saw Thorn at the bottom, standing on what looked like a thin volcanic crust. Out of the cracks came sulphur in yellow puffs of smoke.

"What are you doing down there?"

"How do I know? I was wondering where you had got to."

Amy remembered she had a piece of string in her backpack; she could use it as a rope. After carefully placing her backpack on the ground she pulled out the string. Amy felt like a real live explorer as she held the string and let it fall inside.

"Thorn, grab on and I'll pull you up."

"No, I think you should come down here."

Amy looked around for somewhere to tie the rope. "I can't, Thorn, there's nowhere to tie the rope. What are we going to do?"

Thorn looked at Amy and said, "Move away. I shall do a spell for the rope to hang in mid-air. I love this spell but have never had to use it before."

"Will it work? I don't want to grab onto the rope only for me to fall down. And probably break my back."

"Trust me, Amy. Do you trust me?"

Amy had to think for a moment, and quickly shouted, "Of course I do."

"Well then, hold the rope away from the edge." As Amy held the rope away from the edge, so Thorn began to chant, "Nowhere to tie. But tie high in the sky. Stiff like a pencil. For someone to climb."

Suddenly the rope left Amy's hands and hung stiff as a board in mid-air. Amy grabbed her backpack and slung it around onto her back.

"Cool, it worked. Thorn, it worked!" Amy shouted, jumping up and down in excitement.

Thorn laughed and shouted, "Come on then, you chicken, climb down."

Amy looked at Thorn with a rather cross face and shouted, "I'm no chicken, just a little frightened that I might fall onto my bum, that's all."

"I promise you won't fall. Climb down."

Amy leant over towards the rope, placed one hand onto it and tugged it. She noticed that it stood still so she carefully gripped it with her other hand and placed some of her weight on it.

"Come on already," Thorn impatiently said.

"Okay, I am coming." Amy closed her eyes and began to pull

her legs around the rope. Amy froze for a second and then she began to climb down. She noticed the very funny smell.

"What's that smell?" Amy shouted down.

"Sulphur, Amy, that's all. If you don't hurry up, the spell will wear off and you will fall."

"Okay, okay," mumbled Amy, climbing down now as fast as she could. She thought it would be a good time to open her eyes. She looked down and she could see the bottom. She didn't have far to climb.

"Nearly there," she shouted.

Just as she was almost to the bottom of the crater so the spell wore off. The rope fell, as did Amy, to the floor with a thump.

"Ouch! You knew that was going to happen, didn't you, Thorn?"

Thorn couldn't stop laughing. "I did tell you to hurry. Do you think you could just do that again? I seem to have missed it."

Amy got up and rubbed her bottom, and scowled at poor Thorn, who by this time had stopped laughing.

Chapter Fourteen

AMY LOOKED AROUND. SHE COULD see boulders and rocks everywhere, and the smell of sulphur was strong. She noticed cracks in the ground with puffs of yellow steam that looked like smoke coming from them. Amy felt uneasy about being in a volcano and she turned to Thorn and asked, "Is this volcano about to erupt?"

Thorn looked at Amy and calmly said, "I hope not. This volcano hasn't erupted for over sixty years."

"Thorn, I can't see any pixies or fairies in here. Why do you think we are in here?"

"Don't know, but we must keep searching. There must be a reason; we just haven't found out what it is yet. But we will. I'm sure we will."

Amy looked at Thorn in disbelief and said, "Where do we look first? Just look at this place, it's awful."

As they walked on the volcano's crust, Thorn noticed a crack with a little steam coming from it. Thorn bent down to have a look inside.

"Thorn, what do you think you are doing?" Amy shouted.

"Trying not to get my face burned. Let me concentrate," Thorn scolded. As he bent down, a big puff of steam shot out of the crack. *Psssshhhh*! Thorn moved his face away quickly then he decided to count. "One, two, three." *Psssshhhh* it went again. "Okay, I've worked this out. Every three seconds the steam comes out, which means I can have a quick look."

"That doesn't leave any time at all. We need to stop the steam somehow."

Thorn leant over to the crack, just about to focus when Amy quickly pulled him back.

"Don't be silly, Thorn. Why do you want to look down there so badly anyway?" Amy inquired.

"Don't know. I just have a funny feeling, that's all."

"Thorn, there are cracks in the crust all over the place. You can look down any crack. Why choose the dangerous one? Why?"

"Thought I saw something, that's all."

As Amy followed the jagged line of the crack, it led to another, this time a little wider, without the steam.

"That's better," said a rather pleased Amy. She lay on the ground and peered down into the crack to see what was below. As her eyes began to focus, she was horrified at what she saw. She sat up very sharply and called Thorn. As Thorn came over, Amy looked at him and said, "You were right. You just have to look. Quick, we have to do something! Look, Thorn, look. Hurry; you must hurry."

As Thorn began to lie on the ground he tilted his head to one side and put his eye to the crack. He could see that down below was red lava bubbling away. Hanging down was a long heavy chain with a cage attached to it. In the cage he could see his brother Fern shouting, but no one had been able to hear him due to the noise of the bubbling lava and bursts of escaping steam. The cage looked too close to the lava for Thorn's liking. Thorn sat bolt upright with an extremely straight face.

"How are we going to get my dear brother out?" asked a worried Thorn.

"Let me think."

"No, Amy, we haven't got time to think. The King gave you the gift of wisdom. Use it!"

She began to think but was all flustered. Suddenly she shouted, "USE THE SWORD. See if you can open the crack a bit wider."

Thorn took notice. He began to say, "Sword, open the crack wider." The sword left Thorn's hand and began to turn bronze, slipped into the crack and began to spin. As it slowly spun so the crack began to open up into a big hole.

"STOP!" shouted Thorn.

Just as Thorn commanded, the sword stopped; it hung in mid-air until Thorn gave his next command.

"Sword, come back to my side."

The sword went straight to Thorn and hung back by his side. Thorn and Amy looked down inside the newly made hole. There was a tiny ledge for them to climb down on. As they climbed onto the ledge, Thorn and Amy shouted, "FERN, CAN YOU HEAR US?"

Fern looked up and sighed a sigh of relief, and shouted, "You took your time. What kept you so long?"

"Very funny. We have to get you out of there," shouted Thorn.

They knew they could never grab the chain as it would be too hot, and the heat was unbearable. How has Fern lasted this long, thought Amy?

Thorn turned to Amy and said, "What's that around the cage? It looks like a force field."

As they looked closer they could see a crystal clear blue ball all the way around the cage.

"Hey, Fern, what's that blue ball around the cage?" shouted Amy.

Fern looked up and said, "I made a spell to keep me alive. It's a protective force field to keep me cool, otherwise I would be known as Crispy," laughed Fern.

"Pleased to see you haven't lost your sense of humour. Still the same old Fern, even in a crisis," laughed Thorn.

"You know me, bro. Are you two going to sit on that ledge all day or are you going to get me out of here?" joked Fern.

Amy and Thorn both looked at each other. They knew the chain would be too hot to touch. They also knew that they could never tell the sword to freeze the chain as it would make it too brittle; and it could snap under the weight of the cage and Fern would fall into the lake of lava. They knew they had a big problem. Hmm, they thought.

Thorn took his sword and looked at it and said, "Show me what you can do." The sword immediately left his hand, and cut the chain. The crystal force field accelerated into a spin, holding the cage in mid-air. Thorn covered his eyes as the sword broke through the force field as if cutting into a bubble. Then the sword opened the cage door, and flew down and came to rest at Fern's feet. Fern looked at the sword and wondered what to do. He shouted back to Amy, "What do I do?"

Amy thought for a moment and shouted, "Stand on the blade."

He carefully placed one foot onto the blade wondering if it would fall. The blade stood firm. Fern placed his other foot onto the blade, and to his amazement the sword floated up to the top and set him down safely on the ledge next to his friends. Amy cuddled Fern and grabbed Thorn's arm and said, "Thorn, you can uncover your eyes now. Fern is right here. The sword did it all, it really did it."

Thorn grabbed Fern's arm affectionately as they looked back down to the force field spinning as a ball still suspended in the air. They climbed up from the ledge out of the volcano with pure excitement in their hearts.

"This is a fab sword, you guys. Where did you get it from?" Fern asked.

"The Fairy King," answered Thorn.

"You mean you've met him? I always thought he was an old fairytale. You mean he actually exists?"

"Shame on you, Fern. He's real and beautiful just like the Book describes him."

Fern looked back down past the ledge into the volcano and gazed towards the cage. He spoke and released the blue bubble from around the cage by saying, "Bubble protect and bubble fall, release the cage and protect no more." As the bubble left, so the cage fell into the lava with a splash. Without any warning the ground began to shake; they could hear the lava bubbling in mini explosions. The noise was getting louder than ever and sulphur filled the air.

"RUN!" shouted Fern in a blind panic.

"Where to?" shouted Amy. "We have no way of getting out of this crater."

Thorn told everyone to link hands, and as they did, he lifted the sword in the air and said, "Sword, get us out of here now."

The sword enveloped them in a golden glow and lifted them up out of the crater onto the side of the top of the mountain. Suddenly there was a loud roar and a big explosion; lava came spurting out in all directions from the volcano.

Thorn shouted, "Sword, freeze the lava." The sword glowed blue and froze the lava in mid-air causing a shower of icy rocks to come crashing down.

Thorn shouted, "Sword, protect us." The rocks bounced off an invisible force field.

"Phew, that was lucky," shouted Amy.

"Yes, but we are not safe yet—look!" As they all looked they saw Bones coming up towards them. The sword instantly turned purple and they were all gone. Fern could not believe his eyes. He was staring at the most amazing room he had ever seen. He tapped Amy on her shoulder and asked, "Where are we?"

Amy giggled and said, "The Fairy King's room. His name is Gemstone. You'll see him soon; he has just brought us here."

"Wow! I have never seen a room so beautiful."

To Fern's further surprise he saw his best friends, Marigold and Willow, who were safe. He ran over to them and flung his arms around them both.

"I am so pleased you're okay. I've been so worried."

Chapter Fifteen

A LIGHT, SO BRIGHT THAT IT seemed to consume every-thing, exploded into the room, and within it stood King Gemstone. Amy and Thorn, Marigold and Willow all fell to the ground in respect for the King.

Fern, a little fearful and confused, remained standing, totally unaware of the importance of who had just entered into the room. Amy whispered to Fern, "Kneel, Fern, kneel."

"Why?" he whispered.

"The Fairy King, that's why. Kneel."

Fern was just about to kneel when he heard the gentlest voice ever.

"That's quite alright, Fern, I understand. For I have been watching you for a long time."

"You know my name?" was all Fern could say.

"I know everything about you; I know you never believed in me as do a lot of fairy folk."

"Your Majesty, I am so very sorry."

"You're forgiven. You see, Fern, after I had commissioned your Queen to take care of things by destroying Death and banish-ing him, I had no more need to further intervene in Fairyland. I left my words with you in my Book for you all to study. I did this for you to learn my ways and for you to grow to understand about Fairyland and your King. I gave my Book to your Queen who would teach you in small numbers, and prepare you for this day and for the future. It's only since she has been captured that I am now needed again. I was always watching over you. Just in case you ever needed me. I knew the day was coming when Shadow would attack. I knew that Death would return. For I know all things."

"So why did you let this happen to us then?"

"Fern, watch your mouth!" Willow whispered.

King Gemstone continued. "I have many things for you to know, Fern. Without this day you would never have believed in my power or me. You are one of my chosen few who will fight in the great battle against evil."

"Me? Why me?"

"Why not? I know there is a brave warrior in there. Fern, you didn't give up in that cage because I strengthened you. You survived because you remembered the spell from my Book even though you hadn't truly believed in me."

For once Fern had nothing to say. All he could do was to fall before the King with the rest of them. Totally humble.

"You may arise," commanded the King.

They all stood in complete silence and watched as the King called for Cherry. She is not here, they thought. How does he not know?

Like a bolt out of the sky they all stared in amazement. Cherry was standing before the King. Cherry couldn't believe her eyes; she had to rub them a couple of times just to make sure. As she stared at her King she couldn't help but squeal,"WOW!" She instantly fell to the ground in submission to him.

Gemstone looked at Cherry and smiled and gently said, "You may arise, young one. For I have called you here. This is the time of the gathering of my people to my side, for Shadow's end is near. Amy and Thorn, your battle with Death will soon be upon you. Death is stronger than before so use your gifts wisely and you shall defeat him."

Cherry looked at Gemstone and said, "Your Majesty, where is Oakie? Why is he not here?"

The King looked at Cherry in sympathy and said, "My child, I have left Oakie behind so he can rest, as he cannot yet fly. But the time will come when I will call Oakie to my side."

"Thank you, Your Majesty," said a rather excited Cherry.

Cherry still could not believe that she was in the very room that she had read so much about. It's just like the Book had told us, she thought to herself. Look at how many pictures there are on the walls. All the Fairy Royal Family right back through the ages. Wow!

Amy was just thinking about how well things had gone, when suddenly she thought of her friend Brownie. Sheer panic came over her. Where is Brownie? she thought.

"Ahhh no, we have left him at the volcano. No, oh no … " she began to shout out.

"What's up, my child?" said Gemstone.

"Your Majesty, I am afraid I have been very selfish and I have left my good friend Brownie back at the volcano," sobbed Amy.

Thorn looked at Amy rather puzzled. "Who have we left behind?"

Amy turned to Thorn and said, "We've left Brownie behind, that's who."

Gemstone stepped towards Amy and placed his arm tenderly around her. He smelt like freshly baked cookies. He kindly said, "My child, you have not acted selfishly, not in any way. You have a kind and pure heart thinking of your friend in this way. For Brownie did not go with you to the volcano; I sent only you and Thorn as I knew Brownie wouldn't be needed." The King pointed his finger to the corner of the room and there curled up was Brownie fast asleep, holding his incredibly fat tummy. Amy laughed and sighed in relief.

"Thank you, your Majesty."

Amy ran over to where Brownie was sleeping. She picked him up and held him to her face, and placed a single kiss on his whiskery cheek.

"Here you are, you silly mouse. I was so worried about you. I thought I had left you behind at the volcano."

"Volcano!" shrieked Brownie. "I am pleased I stayed behind then. One thing I hate and that's fire. You see this patch of fur?"

"Yes, what about it? Looks okay to me."

"What about it? Looks okay to you? It's never been the same since it got singed. Just look at it, will you? Okay, is it?" shouted a very disgruntled Brownie. Amy laughed as she could not see the little patch of fur he was talking about.

"You silly mouse, I do love you," said Amy. Brownie snuggled up to Amy, feeling all warm inside.

Chapter Sixteen

NㅤEWS TRAVELLED FAST. WORD HAD got back to Shadow that Thorn and Amy had escaped Death. This had made him very angry. He called one of his top henchmen.

"BONES, BONES, COME HERE NOW!"

Bones quickly came running in. "Yes, boss, what's wrong?"

"WHAT'S WRONG? WHAT'S WRONG? I'LL TELL YOU WHAT'S WRONG!"

"Calm down, boss."

"Calm down? I am furious! That stupid pixie and the girl escaped Death. How?"

"That's not all that escaped, boss."

By this point Shadow had become enraged, with his temper flying high. Bones was very uneasy.

"What do you mean, that's not all that escaped?" he growled. "I command you to talk and do not miss anything out. If I find out that you have missed anything then you shall meet a very nasty death. Do you understand, BONES?"

"Yes, boss, I understand. They have freed two fairies and three pixies. And they have killed two trolls."

"WHAT! This can't have happened; the trees have not blossomed." As he peered into the bubbling cauldron, the mixture began to part in a swirly manner. In the middle, pictures started to form. Shadow could see the trees, and to his surprise, one half of the oak tree had blossomed. This enraged Shadow further.

"How could this be? Only one half of the tree has blossomed.

This must mean Oakie is near, still in Fairyland. We must find him. Guards! Guards! Come here at once."

Snake and Hog came marching in.

"Yes, boss, you yelled?"

"Yes, boys, you are to go to Fairyland and find Oakie. His oak tree has blossomed so he must be near. He might even be in his tree. Search it. Rip Fairyland in two if you have to. Once you have found him, bring him back to me. Now go. Do not come back empty-handed."

"Yes, boss, right away, boss, anything, boss."

Shadow turned towards Bones and said, "You may carry on. So who's the other troll that they've slaughtered."

"Well, boss, they killed Wolf, boss. Word has it, they had a real nasty sword. Thud didn't want to hang around after seeing his friend die in such a nasty and painful way, boss."

"Oh really? Tell me more about this sword. You have my full attention." Shadow leaned in towards Bones and gave him a drink.

"Do tell," said Shadow.

"Well, boss, this sword glows different colours and does all sorts of incredible things. As that pixie stuck it into Wolf, he blew up and just exploded. I've heard, boss, he went out screaming. Yuck! What a way to go. The pixie who carries the sword is said to be one with the sword; they cannot be separated."

"Oh really? We will see about that. You have been most helpful, Bones. You may leave."

Shadow became very interested in the sword. He walked down to his dungeons, looked into a cage, and said sarcastically, "Hello, Queen, long time no see, ha ha. I've just found out about a glowing sword. Tell me more."

"You must be having a laugh. I will never tell you. Never."

"VERY WELL THEN." He reached into the cage and pulled her out. Shadow took the Queen back to where his cauldron was and told her to look into its swirling liquid. Pictures began to appear, showing her Snake and Hog pulling out flowers and trees, destroying the forest.

"NO! STOP!" cried Diamond.

"So you'll tell me, then?"

"NEVER! You'll never get away with this. You will be stopped. Good will always win over evil in the end. And when you lose I will be there to see it."

"Yeah, you reckon. What a fool you are. You think you are actually going to win over me. Look at this." Shadow leant over the cauldron and showed her that Death was back.

"NO! That's impossible; I defeated him and banished him long ago. No, that's not possible."

Shadow began to laugh uncontrollably. "Hahaha!" Catching his breath he snarled and said, "With me everything is possible. You should know that." With that, Shadow got a cage and hung it above his cauldron, and placed Diamond in it and locked the door.

"You, my pretty, will watch Fairyland get ripped to shreds until you tell me how I can get hold of this sword."

Diamond had no option but to watch her precious home being destroyed. My only hope is Amy, she thought, and time is running out. As she looked down into the cauldron she thought she saw some tiny blossom on Oakies's tree. It was then that she knew what they were looking for. Oakie is in great danger, she thought, his tree knows he is in Fairyland and that he is nearby. At least he has been rescued. I must try and reach Oakie with my mind to speak with him and warn him.

The Queen began to think and talk to Oakie.

"Oakie, can you hear me? This is your Queen. You are in great danger; you must get out."

Oakie did not respond to Diamond as he was still too weak to hear her. Having lost both wings he had lost half of his powers too. Diamond was very concerned but was unable to do anything. All she could do was hope.

Chapter Seventeen

KING GEMSTONE STOOD IN SILENCE and then said, "You must go, for I know all things and see all. And I know Oakie is in great danger and needs your help. After you have rescued him, you must bring him back to me. Be careful and use your sword wisely. Keep your eyes on it at all times, for many will try and fool you, and try and steal it from you."

"Yes, your Majesty," they both said.

The King pointed his finger at the wall; then Brownie, Thorn and Amy all disappeared in a beam of light. When they arrived, Thorn noticed that the tables and chairs and all the little acorn cups were scattered everywhere. Plants and trees had been destroyed and uprooted. It was a real mess, heartbreaking to see.

"Wouldn't like to clean this mess up," muttered Brownie.

"This may be a joke to you but this is my home."

"Thorn, I never meant anything by it. Please, that was totally insensitive of me."

Thorn smiled at Brownie as he knew arguing wouldn't help Oakie. As Amy looked around she noticed two trolls up ahead. She also noticed that the spiky snails had gone.

"Mmm. I wonder where they went."

Suddenly, she could hear screaming coming from one of the trolls. He was jumping up and down, and turning round and around in circles. As she looked, she could see he was trying to shake and knock something off himself. What is it? she thought. He is covered in the spiky snails; that's what they are. As she crept closer she could see that they were also stuck to his face and sucking at it. Amy pulled a face, and turned to Thorn and said, "This doesn't make any sense. I thought those snails were Shadow's. So why are they attacking his troll?"

"The snails don't care who works for whom. If anyone goes near them or touches them in any way they will suck their face off. What a way to go."

"Thorn, that's disgusting."

"Easier for us, now we only have one troll to deal with."

"But this is terrible. We need to help him."

"Help him? Why?" shouted Brownie.

"I don't know. I feel sorry for him, that's all," said Amy.

"Would he help you? No he wouldn't, so we will not help him. In fact he would have killed us. So these snails have done us a great favour," Thorn said.

As they turned the corner to go up the path to Thorn's house, they came face to face with Hog.

"Well, well, I was wondering when I would see you lot. In fact I was just about to pay your little friend a visit. Seems that Shadow would like to see him, in a nice big black pot. Now that's funny."

"No!" shouted Amy and Thorn.

As Thorn moved forward, Hog saw something shiny.

"Oh yeah. Is that the sword I've heard so much about? Can do some amazing stuff. Don't look much to me, but I'll take it off you anyway.I hear Shadow will pay a good price for this."

Hog began to swing a big chain above his head; it went so fast that it made a whirling sound. He charged forward and swung it at Thorn, who quickly moved out of the way. He was like lightning; Amy had never seen him move that fast before.

Brownie had a great idea: he needed to get Oakie out without Hog being alerted. He began to tug at Amy's trouser leg. As she bent down he whispered, "I'll run off to Oakie and take him back to the King."

"Brownie, you can't, you don't have the sword to protect you or to take you both back."

"Amy, I have to try before any more trolls come."

"Be careful," she whispered as she watched him scurry up the pebbled path and climb up the side of the house to where the chimney was.

"I just hope he hasn't got his fire lit as I go down, or that will be another patch of fur gone," moaned Brownie. Once he was on top of the roof he could see the whole of Fairyland. One thing he noticed was that it looked bare and dull as he could see everything dying. "Must hurry. I'm sure this place must have been pretty at some time," he stated.

He could also see Thorn just about to draw his sword. "Okay, time for me to jump down this 'ere chimney." He slid down the chimney and landed on the fire grate. Oakie looked shocked to see this tiny mouse in the house.

"Where did you come from, little guy?"

"Less of the little if you don't mind; in this armour I feel about ten feet tall. And I came from your chimney to rescue you."

"Rescue me from what?"

Brownie walked up to Oakie and said in a kind and gentle voice, "I think you need to look out of your window." As Oakie got up and walked over to the window, he was shocked to see half of Fairyland destroyed. And even more surprised at seeing Thorn defending himself against a troll. And at seeing Amy helping him.

"Now you know why I am here. You are in great danger. Shadow has learnt that you have been rescued, and he wants you back. So we have been sent by the Fairy King to take you back to him for you to stay with him until it is safe for you to go back to your tree. We have to defeat Shadow and Death."

"How did Shadow know I had been rescued?"

"Your tree; it had begun to blossom. You must hurry and come with me. Jump on to my back."

Oakie walked over to Brownie and got onto his back. "Come on, I'm ready."

With that Brownie turned tail and ran back up the chimney. Once they reached the top he looked down from the top of the chimney to the roof. Brownie thought it would be best if they stayed where they were. He watched Thorn lift his sword up into the air and swing it hard around his head, shouting, "Sword, do your stuff."

The sword left his hand and went straight into Hog's gut. As it went in it began to turn around and around, and glow black. Thorn had never seen it do that before. As it glowed, so Hog began to scream; his whole body puffed up and began to swell and swell. Thorn and Amy backed off, cringing; they knew that he was about to blow. But instead he grew bigger and bigger. He began to float upwards. Panic was in his eyes, and he was screaming louder and louder as he floated straight past Brownie, until suddenly ... BANG!

The sword fell to the ground but there was no sign of Hog. He had disappeared—blown into a million little pieces. Brownie and Oakie began to cheer from the top of the chimney, catching Amy's attention.

"Hey, Thorn, look up there." As Thorn looked up, there to his surprise was the little mouse with his best friend. Thorn began to wave and beckoned them down. Brownie felt brave and triumphant. He wanted to jump down in victory; he felt he could do it this time; he had always wanted to see what it would feel like to have the wind blowing in his fur as he fell through the air. Just this once, he thought. He walked over to the edge of the roof with Oakie holding tightly to his back and jumped. As he jumped, Thorn became very worried for his two little friends.

He held his sword up into the air and shouted, "TAKE US BACK TO THE KING, QUICK!" The sword glowed purple just as Brownie had jumped half way down; he had nearly reached them. And just when he was beginning to experience what it was like to have the wind in his fur, they were gone … and back in the safety of the King's room.

"What did you do that for? My lifelong dream, gone in a flash!" moaned Brownie.

"You are a rather funny little mouse, aren't you?" laughed Amy.

The King rose from his throne to meet the four. Brownie was still complaining about the jump.

"Is everything alright, Brownie?"

"Oh yes, Your Majesty, I was just talking to myself, that's all."

"Very well. I see you have brought Oakie back to us safely."

"Yes, Your Majesty, but half of Fairyland was destroyed. There was nothing we could do to stop that."

"I am fully aware of that. I need you to go back to Fairyland and get the Big Book. I fear it will not be safe much longer, and the secrets of Fairyland will be exposed and used for evil."

"Yes, Your Majesty," they all shouted.

As he looked at them he gently said, "Be gone."

Chapter Eighteen

THEY FOUND THEMSELVES STANDING BACK in the middle of Fairyland.

"Can't say I am getting used to this teleporting stuff," grumbled Brownie.

As they made their way to Diamond's castle, Amy thought she saw something run past.

"What was that?"

"What was what?" replied Thorn.

"I don't know. I thought I saw something run past us, that's all. We must be on our guard." Amy held her shield up ready for any unexpected unwanted visitors. Thorn looked at Amy and drew his sword just to be on the safe side. After all, Amy did have the gift of wisdom.

They carried on walking until they came to Diamond's castle. Amy grabbed Thorn's arm and pulled him back, and said, "Wait. Something is wrong. I can feel it."

"Of course something is wrong. The whole place is ruined."

As Thorn opened the big door, they were met by the Fairy King. Amy began to get suspicious; she just knew that something was wrong. She thought she would play along just to see what would happen. One question she had running around her head was, why would the Fairy King come here himself? It didn't make any sense. Amy whispered in her head, "Thorn, be careful." Thorn looked at Amy as if she were mad and greeted the King in the normal manner.

"Your Majesty, what are you doing here? We have only just left you."

"Yes, I know you have, and I am very grateful that you are all so obedient to my commands. But I forgot to recharge your sword. May I have a look at it?"

The King stretched out his arm towards Thorn waiting for him to place the sword into his hand. Amy looked at Thorn and thought, recharge the sword? This sword doesn't need to be recharged. Thorn, who was convinced that this was the King, was just about to place the sword in his hand when Amy shouted, "WAIT!" Everyone looked at her.

"Why does the sword need to be recharged? Everyone knows that this sword doesn't need to be recharged."

This made the King very angry. "ARE YOU QUESTIONING ME, GIRL?"

Amy knew she had to be strong for Thorn, as he was completely gullible. She could see that Thorn was about to make the biggest mistake of his life, so she bravely said, "YES, I am questioning you."

The King was enraged. "How dare you! You shall pay for this. Thorn, your power will be gone from the sword if you don't let me recharge it. NOW GIVE IT TO ME!"

Thorn's hand began to shake as he nervously stretched out his arm towards the King. He was now a little unsure so he held the handle of the sword very tightly. Amy leapt forward, placing her hand on top of the sword, and said boldly to the King, "You do realise if you're not the King and you hold this sword you will instantly be burned alive."

Brownie suddenly understood what Amy was thinking. Now he was on the same page as her. Sniff, sniff, sniff, he smelt the King. He could smell a smell that wasn't cookies. Brownie now knew that Thorn was about to make the worst decision of his life. It was now or never; he was not about to watch his friend make such a big mistake. He shouted, "STOP!"

Just as the King was about to take the sword, it began to show a reflection. The reflection shone so brightly it dispersed the deception. Thorn looked at his sword in shock; he could see this was no King, but an evil troll. Thorn quickly pulled the sword back; and as he did so, the King changed into Furball, his true identity. Thorn felt so stupid. How could he have not known?

"I thought he was the King, I really did!"

Amy felt so sorry for Thorn but this was not the time to have a meaningful conversation. Furball stomped forward, hitting his club in his hand; he was really mad, with steam coming from his nose and white froth coming from his mouth. With each step so he began to grow, and as he grew, so fur grew all over him.

"Now I know why they call him Furball," Amy said with a rather straight face.

"I am really mad now," he growled. "You shouldn't have angered the Furball."

Opening his mouth wide, he spurted fire at them. Huge flaming balls of fur came flying towards them with such a force. Thorn held the sword to one side and batted the flames back at him. The flames bounced off the sword straight back at Furball. He looked fearfully at them and tried to knock them out of his way, but his fur instantly caught fire, and as he went up in flames he ran and rolled about, screaming in agony, trying to put the flames out, but he went up in a blaze.

"Quick!" said Amy. "Tell the sword to put him out. This is too horrible. Do something!"

Thorn held his sword in the air and shouted, "Freeze this Furball!" The sword instantly glowed blue, and the room became very cold. Amy's teeth began to chatter. As they looked at Furball, they saw him completely turn to ice. Thorn laughed and swung his sword into the now frozen Furball, shouting, "This is for tricking me." He shattered Furball into a million pieces. Thorn turned to Amy and hung his head in shame. All he could say was, "I am sorry. And thanks, you guys, for saving me."

"We didn't save you; we just stopped you from making a big mistake, that's all."

"Well, thanks anyway."

"You're welcome," shouted Brownie.

As they ran down the long brightly-coloured corridor they came to the room where the Big Book lay. It sat there with such importance! This Book was the fairies' lives; all that was in Fairyland was because of this Book. Thorn didn't want to touch it. No one had even taken it off its stand before. Amy looked at Thorn and said, "You do know that you shouldn't be in awe of this Book, but of the one who wrote it. Shall I take it off the stand, or are we going to keep staring at it?"

"Yes, please," said a rather nervous Thorn.

As Amy picked the Book up, so it began to ask, "Where are we going, Amy? My home is here. It has been for thousands of years, long before you were ever born." The Book paused for a second and said, "For it is not I who wrote the words within me, young Thorn, but the King. It is him you should be in awe of, not me. But only a child of pure heart with the gift of wisdom could see that. Amy, you are indeed the chosen one."

"Thank you. You are so kind, but I fear we are in great danger. We need to get you back to the Fairy King as soon as possible. Shadow could be watching us or even listening to our every word."

"Thank you, young Amy."

"You're welcome," Amy said politely.

Amy couldn't help but feel a little weird; she had never spoken to a book before, let alone to a book that talked back. Thorn held the sword in the air but this time, before he could even say a thing, they were gone. In a flash they were back in the Throne Room, and Amy handed the Book to King Gemstone.

"Your Majesty, as you have requested, your Book."

"I trust that the mission went well?" said the King as he took the Book.

Thorn knew in his heart that the King knew what had happened, for the King knew all things. Amy smiled and nudged Thorn forward, and as Thorn stepped forward he blurted out, "I nearly gave the sword up. I thought it was you, honestly."

Amy thought it would be best for her to explain as Thorn seemed to be struggling to get his words out.

"Your Majesty, when we arrived at the castle, we were met by what looked to us like you. He told Thorn that he needed the sword to recharge it as it would lose its power. It was a simple mistake."

"I know. Young Thorn, as I told you earlier, many will try and steal it. And many will come in my name to trick you. The sword will never lose its power, unless I take its power from it. The sword will protect you, and will accomplish everything that is within my will. Amy had known this as she had used her gift wisely. You did well, Thorn, don't worry. The sword revealed Furball's reflection. Outwardly, he appeared to be me, but inwardly the sword revealed his ugliness. The sword reveals the truth and the truth will always set you free."

The King pointed at them and the three were gone.

Chapter Nineteen

AS THEY ARRIVED, THEY STARTED to wonder where they were. As Amy looked around she could see fields that went on for miles. At the end of the field that they were in there seemed to be a cornfield. Brownie got very excited. He loved fields; his nose went straight into the air and started to sniff the fresh air. As he sniffed he began to cough and cough.

"What's wrong, Brownie? Are you feeling okay?" Amy began to gently pat him on his back to help him.

Suddenly Thorn began to smell something.

"That's awful. Cover your mouth; whatever you do you must not breathe this in. Look!" As Thorn pointed in front of him they could see black smog emerging, covering the whole of the next field. Amy noticed that it was killing all the flowers and trees, and any living thing it touched.

"What is it, Thorn? And what's that smell?" asked Amy, now very worried for her good friend Brownie, who was still coughing uncontrollably.

"We need to find a safe place."

"But where? There is nothing but fields here. Thorn, we need to hurry otherwise Brownie won't make it. He seems to be having trouble breathing," said a very muffled Amy, who was still covering her mouth. They frantically looked around, but found nothing. The sword began to glow a bright brown. As it glowed so it left Thorn's side and began to tunnel underground. As they watched, they could see the sword going further and further down. Thorn started to get worried as he could see the black smog spreading to where they were. He looked into the hole. As he did, he was very surprised to see that the sword had tunnelled and made a room underneath them. Thorn looked up and shouted in a panic for them to follow him.

As Thorn climbed into the hole so the sword floated up to meet him. Thorn stepped onto the sword; as he did, he noticed that it had begun to expand in length and width. Thorn was amazed; this sword could do anything. He waited for the others to follow.

"Hurry up, you two, we're running out of time. Look."

As Amy looked back she could see the smog moving faster and faster towards them, killing everything in its path.

"Come on, Brownie, you can do it."

"No, you must go on without me; I am too weak to move. I feel my chest is about to cave in. You must hurry," coughed a very wheezy mouse.

Amy could feel tears welling up; her throat became tight and burned where she was trying to fight back the tears. She grabbed Brownie and held him in her arms; she wriggled down the hole and onto the sword. The sword began to slowly move down, and as it did, Amy could see the black smog covering the ground where they had just been. Down they went into the newly dug underground cave. Once they had reached the bottom, the sword regained its normal size.

"Wow," said Thorn.

Amy laid Brownie onto the ground. "There you go, little fella."

Brownie just lay there; he didn't move. His eyes were closed and his mouth was half open; his breathing was very shallow. Amy feared the worst. A single tear ran from Amy's cheek and fell into Brownie's mouth. Amy looked up at Thorn and said, "I think we've lost him, I think he's dead."

Amy cried uncontrollably. Thorn noticed that Brownie's breathing had become faster and his mouth was moving as if he was drinking. But what is he drinking? thought Thorn. As he looked up he noticed that Amy's tears were going into Brownie's mouth.

"That's it!" Thorn shouted, which startled Amy. As Amy looked she noticed a rather excited pixie in front of her. "LOOK!" shouted Thorn, pointing to Brownie. "Look what your tears are doing".

As Amy looked down she could see Brownie moving and having a wash as if he had just woken up after a nap. Amy grabbed Brownie and gave him a big kiss.

"Oh, Brownie, you're okay, you're really okay."

A very confused Brownie said, "Er, yes, I'm fine. Why do you ask such a strange question? Mind you, I do have a very sore throat. Would anyone like to explain? And why are we in a big dirty cave? It's going to take ages for me to lick all this dirt off."

Amy and Thorn both laughed and said, "He's back." Amy looked at Thorn and asked why her tears had made Brownie better.

"Better? Was I ill then? I really don't remember," said a rather puzzled mouse.

Thorn began to explain that in the Book "it is said that the one who is chosen shall have tears of magic, and when her tears fall to the ground so they shall heal".

Amy had a question. "How do you know what is in the Book if no one was allowed to touch it? How do you know all this?"

Thorn put his hand on Amy's shoulder and said, "Only our Queen had ever handled the Book, only she has been given authority to read from it, only she is worthy. She would read the words of the Book to us. And we would have the words written on our hearts forever."

"Wow, that's really beautiful, Thorn."

"I know, Amy. This was our world before all this happened. We must continue."

Amy was so pleased that Brownie was okay, but one thing

was still puzzling her. "What was that black smog? And what was that smell?"

Thorn turned to Amy as if to say, you really want to know? Amy looked at Thorn and blurted out, "Yes I do. I have the right to know."

"Very well then. The smell that almost killed Brownie was the smell of burning sulphur. It gets into your lungs and fills them with gas and slowly kills you. The black smog was Death; he roams the ground looking for living things to devour and as he kills them so he draws power from them. That's why we had to get Brownie out of there; if we had left him behind then Death would have swallowed him up, and who knows what power he would have got from him? One thing is for sure: Death is getting bigger and stronger by the second and he must be stopped, otherwise nothing will survive." Thorn looked at his sword and said, "Take us up to the top."

Instead of the sword taking them back as requested, it began to show a picture in the blade of the field above. The field was ruined; everything around it was gone, withered away. Thankfully, there was no sign of Death; he had completely disappeared. The sword began to hover in the air and expand in length and width once more. The three of them stepped onto it and they were taken back up to the surface. As they looked around, it was the most dreadful sight they had ever seen. The flowers and the trees had not only lost their colour, but had died. The grass was no longer green and lush, but brown and withered and burned. They all looked at each other, unable to speak.

As they carried on walking, making their way to the cornfield, instead of seeing lovely yellow corn they saw it was filled with black smoke; the corn had been completely burnt up, with nothing remaining.

"Oh no, this is terrible," said Amy.

"Yeah," replied Thorn.

As they were walking they came to a hole in the ground. They all stopped and looked at one another.

"What do you think this is for?" Brownie asked.

"Take a good look, Thorn; see what you think it is for," said Amy.

Thorn got on his stomach and looked into the hole but it was too dark to see.

"I need a torch." Amy passed her torch to him; he took the torch and shone it down into the hole. As the light hit the ground so it reflected two shiny lights.

Thorn shouted, "Hello? Anyone there?"

All of a sudden, a little trembling voice said, "H ... hello, my name is Narna."

"Narna, can we come down? Is it safe?" asked Thorn.

"Yes, you can. Please come on down."

Thorn sat the sword over the hole; the sword started to rotate and began to make the hole bigger. Once it had finished, the three of them stepped onto the sword, and it lowered them into the hole. When they reached the bottom they could see a tiny little lantern flickering in the corner giving barely enough light to see. Thorn began to call for Narna; a very frightened voice said, "I am over here." Thorn pointed his torch into the corner. To his surprise and great joy he saw a mouse, and huddled up to the mouse was Corn. Thorn thought he was seeing things. He rubbed his eyes and shone the torch again. There they were both huddled up together.

"Corn, you're safe! But how?" asked Thorn.

Corn was very pleased to see his friend; he got up and hugged Thorn.

"Where are my manners? This is my new friend, Narna. She rescued me."

"But how? And where?" answered a very puzzled Thorn.

As Narna came out of the corner, she brushed herself down and explained. "This field above was once my home with all my brothers and sisters and friends. We all used to play and eat in the lush cornfields; we used to have such fun.

"One day we were all out having fun, eating and playing, when this black smog started to appear. We had no idea what it was. Some of us got scared and ran away; the rest of my family stayed and were killed by this smog as they stood there just staring at it."

"So there are more of you?" asked Amy.

Narna looked at Amy and shook her head in sadness.

"The rest of my friends got killed looking for my family. When I saw the smog coming I started to dig this tunnel under the cornfield. In my panic I went the wrong way and accidentally tunnelled upwards, hitting a dead end. I frantically dug around to get past what was in my way, and found myself above ground again looking at Corn in a big cage. The door was locked so I used my tail to pick the lock. I could see the black smog almost upon us so I grabbed Corn and took him down the hole. I couldn't leave him; not out there. Since then, he has been helping me fill in the other hole and we have built another tunnel, which leads into another field with a stream that we have been drinking from. We have lived here until now," explained Narna.

Thorn could not believe his ears. All he could say to Narna was, "Thank you and I'm so sorry for your great loss."

Brownie, who was rather impressed with Narna, pushed past Amy and introduced himself to her.

"I am Brownie. Pleased to meet you. You must come back with us."

"Pleased to meet you too, Brownie, and I would love to come with you. I have made a good friend in Corn and I would not want to be without him." Corn placed his hand onto Narna's head and ruffled her fur.

"Ok, then, it's time to go." Thorn lifted his sword up into the air and said, "Back to the King." The sword glowed purple and took them back.

The King bent down to Narna and picked her up and said, "So who do we have here, then?"

Narna looked at the King with her big brown eyes and nervously said, "Narna, sir, my name is Narna. I have become friends with Corn."

Corn stepped forward and bravely stated, "She saved my life; I would be dead if it was not for her. Shadow had left me out in the open for Death to kill me. She's not only my friend but a hero."

The King put her down and smiled a kind and gentle smile.

"Very well. She will wear the armour to protect her on her journey. Now it is time."

He pointed his hand, and in a beam of light they were gone.

Chapter Twenty

THEY FOUND THEMSELVES BACK IN the field next to the cornfield. They could see in the distance the black smog emerging from the ground, sucking the life out of anything that might have survived. Amy looked at Thorn and said, "What are we doing back here? Something must have gone wrong."

"The King's never wrong, but I feel our mission wasn't complete. We have missed something. I know we have," shouted Thorn.

"But what?" shouted Amy, who was now getting very worried as the black smog was creeping towards them.

"Follow me; I can take you back to my den," shouted Narna. They turned around and saw the smog coming after them. "Are you going to follow me or not?" shouted a rather impatient mouse.

They all began to run towards the slope that Narna and Corn had built. They were almost there when Amy tripped badly and fell. Rolling around in agony, she grabbed her knee in pain and saw that it was bleeding. "I can't stand!" she shrieked. Amy could feel those big red eyes burning into her back.

"We have to get her into the hole!" shouted Thorn.

"But how? She's far too heavy for us."

"I don't know, Brownie, but one thing I do know is that Death is gaining on us fast."

Thorn looked down and had a great idea: he took the sword

and shouted, "Take us to safety." As soon as he said it, they were safe in the hole. Thorn stood at the edge of the slope and lay on his stomach. He could see Death sucking the last little bit of life out from the ground. He was amazed to see the earth die so quickly and fill Death with so much power; as he grew bigger he turned darker. His eyes seemed to become redder.

How are we ever going to stop him? thought Thorn. He crawled deeper in the hole to rejoin the others. He looked at Amy and said, "Are you okay?"

"I'll live, thanks."

They could all see something was troubling Thorn. Brownie walked over to Thorn and said, "What's up? You looked bothered"

Thorn took a deep breath and said, "We still have Blossom to rescue and we're stuck in here."

Suddenly the ground began to shake. Thorn looked at the others and whispered, "Sword, show us the outside." The sword began to glow and pictures began to form. They all gathered around the sword, eager to find out what was happening outside. As the picture began to get clearer so they saw Death right above them, sucking the ground with something held tight in his hand. But what was it? They couldn't quite make it out. Thorn told the sword to focus on Death's hand. As the sword did so they made a very shocking discovery. As they stared at his hand, Thorn whispered, "He has Blossom; he knows we are here. We have to help her, but how?"

The sword glowed a bright green and red. They had never seen it do that before. Suddenly, the King's face appeared in the sword. They all looked at each other, and back at the sword, expecting the image to be gone, but to their amazement, he was still there.

"My children, time is running out! The time has come for you go into battle. You are to be strong and courageous. Use the sword; it will help you in your time of need. Fear not, for I am with you. The time will come when I shall return."

The picture began to fade. They all looked at each other

with terror in their eyes. They got up and walked up the slope in complete silence. As Thorn put his hand on the metal handle of his sword, his leg went back as he stood in a fighting stance. He glared at Death. Death turned and faced them, laughing. He towered above them, moving closer and closer with every step, the ground pounding with his every move. Brownie could now see that Blossom was held tightly in his hand.

"How are we going to get her out of his hand, Thorn?"

"I don't know. Can't say I've thought about it," Thorn snapped as he could see Death virtually face to face. Thorn look at his sword and said, "I don't know if you can do what I am about to ask, but here goes anyway." He took hold of the sword, held it high in the air, and shouted, "Sword, heal and give Blossom the strength to break free from the grip of Death."

They all stared at the sword, waiting for it to glow but nothing happened. Thorn felt very disheartened. He looked at Amy and said, "I knew it wouldn't work."

"That's *it*! That's why it didn't work," Amy shouted.

"What's *it*, Amy? What are you talking about?" Thorn, who was now very worried about their safety, began to shout, "RUN, RUN NOW!" The four of them looked around and saw Death reaching out for them. His big black hand swooped down to kill them. Their hearts were pounding; pure fear was running through their veins. His clenched fist pounded the ground, just missing them.

Amy looked at Thorn and shouted in panic, "We're running out of time. You must believe in your heart, or nothing will work." Thorn could hear the King's voice, saying, "Be courageous."

Thorn held the tall blade in the air and shouted, "Sword, heal and give Blossom strength to break free from Death." As they watched the sword, it left his hand and a brilliant white light glowed from the tip of the blade. It shone so brightly that the rays began to penetrate deep into Death. Immediately he began to yell in a deep gruff voice, "NOOOOOOO!" He instantly let go of Blossom but was fixed to one spot. He could not move.

Battle

Blossom fell to the floor, not wanting to look back. She ran as fast as she could. She ran over to Amy and the others, and shouted in her loudest voice, "Can we go?"

As soon as she spoke she was gone. Amy looked around in a panic and said, "Where is she? Brownie, did you see where Blossom went?"

Brownie began to look round. He sniffed the air to see if he could get her scent. He looked at Amy and shook his head, and said, "Nope, she's not around here."

They could see fear deep in Death's eyes as more rays of light beamed from the blade and penetrated into him. Death began to shrink, and as he shrank, he shouted, "I'll get you for this; I am not finished with you yet."

Thorn grinned at him and shouted, "Sword, do your thing." The sword began to spin. As it spun it went straight into Death's evil black heart. More screams filled the air as the sword drove him into the ground and he was gone. The sword came to rest with the blade firmly in the ground.

Thorn carefully walked over to the sword, placing his hands onto the metal handle. His hands gripped it firmly, and pulled it from the ground. As it came out of the ground so Thorn heard Death's final scream. He clutched the sword and ran to where the others were still standing.

"Where is she?" said Thorn, looking around for Blossom.

Amy looked at Thorn, shrugged her shoulders, and said, "I don't know. She disappeared after she escaped."

The sword began to talk to prepare them for their next task and that was to defeat Shadow and rescue Diamond. They all looked at each other; in their eyes they looked scared. They knew this day would come; they knew it had to arrive. They looked at the sword and said, "Take us to Shadow's castle." They all held hands, and Brownie and Narna held paws, and then they were gone.

Diamond, from within the cage, had been watching everything, looking down into Shadow's cauldron. She was delighted to see Death defeated and all the pixies and fairies safe in the King's hands. She could see that Amy and Thorn and the mice were in the castle on their way to rescue her. She thought, I have to help them stay undetected. She wondered what the cauldron would do if she spoke to it. She looked at the picture and whispered, "Show me Fairyland."

The picture began to change just in time as she could hear footsteps echoing down the long dark corridor. Shadow stormed into the room and peered into his cauldron at the picture below. He began to laugh; a loud gruff laugh.

"Perfect, just perfect. Look, Diamond, your home has been destroyed and not a hero in sight."

The Queen peered into the cauldron and could see that Fairyland was indeed destroyed. She felt happiness as she knew Shadow was about to be in for a very big surprise, but a heavy sadness began to well up in her heart as she looked at Fairyland.

"No good crying now. I have won. Fairyland is finally mine. Your power will be all mine once I drain all your powers from you."

Diamond began to laugh and said, "Fairyland will never be yours; you will never have my power! Have you asked the cauldron where Amy and Thorn are?"

Shadow's face began to change as he quickly said, "Show me Amy and Thorn." The picture began to change; Shadow could see them inside the castle, climbing the big stone spiral staircase up to the very top. He could see Thorn carrying the sword and using it as a light to guide them. Shadow's face changed, and he looked at Diamond and said, "Tell me more about that sword or you will die."

"You will never kill me, and you will never own that sword for it has chosen its owner, and it's not you!" shouted Diamond.

This made Shadow furious. He grabbed Diamond out of the cage and held her over the boiling cauldron.

"You will tell me how I can get that sword or you will meet your death."

"Shadow, your Death creature has been defeated. So you are

running out of time and helpers," laughed a very nervous Queen, hanging upside down looking at the green bubbling pot, wondering if she had gone a little too far. Flashbacks of her life flew before her eyes. A single tear ran from her eye as she thought to herself that she had let everyone down. As the tear slowly fell into the hot liquid it started to sparkle, only enough for the Queen to notice. Her tear began to slowly freeze the bottom of the mixture. Shadow was just about to drop her into what he thought would be his boiling pot when he heard, "Leave her alone, Shadow." Shadow turned around and laughed.

"I've been expecting you two and that sword. You give me that sword and I shall give her to you. No sword, no Queen."

Thorn could see her hanging upside down over the pot. Half of him was screaming NO, never, but he wanted to save his precious Queen.

Amy looked at Thorn and quickly said, "No, Thorn, no. Diamond wouldn't want you to give that sword away, especially not to him."

Thorn looked at Amy and hung his head in shame and quietly said, "I have to, if I want to save our Queen; then I will be able to save Fairyland."

"No, no! Don't you understand? If you give him the sword there won't be a Fairyland," Amy said in a rather stern voice. "We've come too far now. Don't give up."

Shadow looked at her and shouted, "BE QUIET, YOU STUPID GIRL. For your stupidity the Queen will die." He slowly released his fingers off her legs. Thorn was horrified as he watched his beloved Queen begin to fall into the pot. Her screams echoed through the castle.

"NOOOOO!" shouted Thorn. "I'll throw you the sword."

Shadow laughed and caught the Queen's leg, his eyes bulging out of his head with pure excitement running through his veins. Thorn looked at the sword and said, "I'm sorry I have let you all down."

"Give it to me, boy," shouted Shadow. Thorn looked at Amy with tears in his eyes and threw the sword to Shadow. As it went hurtling through the air, Shadow reached up and caught it.

Chapter Twenty-One

As Shadow stood there with the sword, he looked up to the ceiling and said, "I feel the power of the sword running through my veins. I feel powerful, more powerful than I have ever before." As he held Diamond in his hand he brought her up to his face and said, "I no longer need you, or your power, for I have greater power now."

He released his grip and dropped her into the black pot, laughing uncontrollably, and saying, "You fools, I have completed my task, for now I shall reign and rule over you all, hahaha." Shadow gazed at the sword, admiring its beauty.

Thorn quickly flew over to the pot with tears streaming down his face, shouting, "I'm sorry, I'm sorry. I've let you all down, I know I have."

As he peered into the pot, to his surprise he saw the Queen lying on the ice. As she looked up she smiled a sweet smile, put a finger over her mouth, and said, "Ssshh." Thorn had never been so relieved. After making sure that Shadow wasn't looking, he quietly flew down inside the pot and reached out to Diamond and gently took hold of her hand. Nervously he looked up; he had to make sure that Shadow hadn't seen them. Once he knew it was all clear he helped the Queen out of the pot. Shadow had become mesmerised looking at the sword, relishing its power. He shouted, "Say goodbye to your Queen, and say hello to your new and powerful King." Shadow raised the sword and said, "Kill Fairyland."

Everyone was waiting for the sword to glow or do something different, but nothing happened; instead, loud music began to play. Amy looked at Thorn and said, "Thorn, what's happening? Why is it doing that?"

"Don't know. It's never happened to us."

As they watched, Shadow began to get very worried as he looked at the sword, wondering what was happening. The music got louder and louder as if it were coming nearer. The Queen whispered to Thorn, "Look up."

As Thorn and Amy looked up into the sky they had never seen anything like it. The King was coming out of the sky with all the fairies and pixies they had rescued and countless more. Their colours were spectacular; they were all flying on white unicorns. The King had a golden rod in one hand and the Big Book in the other and on his head was a big golden crown. All the fairies had golden crowns too. The sight was truly awesome.

As they got closer Amy shouted, "Shadow, look up; meet your destiny."

As Shadow looked up fear struck him. He wanted to run away but somehow his feet were glued to the floor. As the King and his army landed the castle walls disappeared, everything in the room was gone. The King walked over to Shadow and said firmly, "You were made perfectly, you had a wonderful life. But you chose evil, you chose the foolish things, you became greedy and self-centred, your heart became hard and dark, you chose to hate children as well as your own kind. You tricked young Thorn into thinking that he would save his Queen if he gave you the sword, but you lied and chose evil again. The sword will not give you power, as it knows when it's in the hands of the evil one. The moment you had the sword you again chose evil. Shadow, you chose not to live by my words in this Book. I will be banishing you to a dark place where you can never harm anyone or anything again."

The King raised his hand and pointed to the ground. The

ground opened up into a dark pit. Shadow, who was now looking at the pit, was shouting, "Please, Your Majesty, please don't send me down there. I beg your forgiveness."

"Forgiveness is not granted. It is too late. Now begone with you."

As the King spoke, so Shadow was gone. When Amy and Thorn looked into the pit they saw Shadow tied in chains and screaming. The King pointed his hand to the ground and said, "Ground, close and let Shadow never escape." The ground shut tight with a bang. Diamond came forward and bowed before the King and said, "Thank you, Your Majesty."

"You're welcome. Come, let us all go back."

In a flash they were standing in Fairyland, looking at what Shadow had done. The King walked forward and said, "Let the trees stand again, make everything new." To Amy's surprise the trees were back in their holes, the tables and chairs back in their places. But most of all she noticed the colour slowly coming back into the trees and flowers as their fairies returned to them. The grass became pure green again and the streams ran like crystal. Everything was restored. Diamond stood next to the King. Her dress was beautiful; diamonds covered the front of it, with sequins mixed in. She had crystal shoes on her feet and a tiny golden crown on her head. She stepped forward and placed one hand on Thorn's shoulder and another one on Amy's.

"You are my brave warriors; you risked your own lives to save others and our home. We are truly thankful to you both."

The Queen stepped back, and the King stepped forward and placed his golden rod onto Amy's shoulder and said, "Amy, you will be given a new name; you will be known as Brave Warrior. We will call you by our golden trumpet; and you will hear it for I give you the gift of fairy hearing, and you will be ready for service. I place this silver crown upon your head to show how brave you have been.

King Gemstone and Queen Diamond

"And, Thorn, I place a silver crown onto your head for you also were very brave. And to Brownie and Narna, I give you a tiny gift of cheese for your bravery too. And to Oakie … please step forward, young pixie."

Oakie nervously stepped forward and bowed in front of the King. The King looked at him and said, "Arise. I will give you the gift of new wings, for you didn't give any secrets away, and you sacrificed your wings for us."

The King placed his rod onto Oakie's back and new wings began to grow. Oakie was so pleased he hugged the King and said, "Thank you, Your Majesty."

The King turned back to Amy and said, "Amy, it is time for you to go back through the Magical Gate now. You must return back to your world. The moment you step back though the Gate two things will happen. The first is, you will regain your usual size. The second is, time will return to normal."

Amy felt sad that she was leaving but glad that their world was back to normal. She turned around and one by one hugged them all. As she walked back through the beautiful and peaceful countryside of Fairyland the Magical Gate appeared. She took one more look around before she went through it. She opened the Gate and went through. Just as the King had said, she had regained her usual size. Amy felt weird being back to normal again. She quietly walked back to her bedroom and lay on her bed. She looked at the clock as it began to tick; she knew her mission was complete. And a new one was about to begin.

About the Author

Julie Earle was born in 1976 and raised in Luton, England. Her father told her fairy stories from his own imagination which captivated her into a world of fantasy. As she grew up she took her imaginative skills to school and got her first story published in the school magazine. After leaving school Julie worked in a small playgroup filling children's imaginations with all her stories. She loved working with children and later went onto college and received a diploma in Nursery Nursing. Still with a very creative imagination, she was able to share stories with the many children that she worked with.

She now lives in Essex with her husband and four children. Her passion for writing took over and she became a member of a freelance writers' group. Many people told her to begin writing for children as they could see she enjoyed telling stories. After having her fourth child, Julie began to create *The Magical Gate* book; and so it was born. Out of the imagination of this young woman comes a reality that grips every reader. She hopes you will get as much enjoyment reading it as she did writing it.